NERD CAMP

ELISSA BRENT WEISSMAN

Atheneum Books for Young Readers

New York London Toronto Sydney New Delhi

ATHENEUM BOOKS FOR YOUNG READERS
An imprint of Simon & Schuster Children's Publishing Division
1230 Avenue of the Americas, New York, New York 10020

This book is a work of fiction. Any references to historical events, real people,
or real locales are used fictitiously. Other names, characters, places, and incidents
are products of the author's imagination, and any resemblance to actual events
or locales or persons, living or dead, is entirely coincidental.

For information about special discounts for bulk purchases, please contact
Simon & Schuster Special Sales at 1-866-506-1949 or business@simonandschuster.com.
The Simon & Schuster Speakers Bureau can bring authors to your live event. For more
information or to book an event, contact the Simon & Schuster Speakers Bureau
at 1-866-248-3049 or visit our website at www.simonspeakers.com.
Also available in an Atheneum Books for Young Readers hardcover edition
Book design by Jessica Handelman and Karina Granda
The text for this book is set in Cheltenham.
Manufactured in the United States of America
0615 OFF
First Atheneum Books for Young Readers paperback edition May 2012
6 8 10 9 7 5
The Library of Congress has cataloged the hardcover edition as follows:
Weissman, Elissa Brent.
Nerd camp / Elissa Brent Weissman. — 1st ed.
p. cm.
Summary: For ten-year-old Gabe, the Summer Center for Gifted Enrichment is all that
he dreamed it would be, but he must work hard to write about the fun in letters to Zach,
his cool future stepbrother, without revealing that it is a camp for "nerds."
ISBN 978-1-4424-1703-8 (hc)
[1. Camps—Fiction. 2. Ability—Fiction. 3. Stepbrothers—Fiction.
4. Interpersonal relations—Fiction. 5. Individuality—Fiction.] I. Title.
PZ7.W448182Ner 2011
[Fic]—dc22 2010042913
ISBN 978-1-4424-1704-5 (pbk)
ISBN 978-1-4424-1705-2 (eBook)

For my grandparents,
Joan, Marty, Terry, and Lee:
I'm one lucky nerd to have your
never-ending support

NERD CAMP

Chapter 1
GABE

It was so late that it was almost tomorrow. Gabe had been awake later than this only once before. That was New Year's Eve, and his mom had let him have a sleepover with some of his math team friends. Rather than counting down to the new year when it was just ten seconds away, like most people, at 8:00 p.m. they figured out how many seconds there were until the ball dropped and then counted down ten seconds occasionally throughout the night (at 8:32 they counted down from 12,480 to 12,470).

He thought now of figuring out how many seconds there were until his train tomorrow, but that would probably just make him more excited and anxious, and Gabe needed to *stop* thinking about tomorrow so he could sleep.

He couldn't help being excited about the future—*the future with my new brother!* he thought, even though he was trying so hard *not* to think at all. He remembered back to first grade, when his friend Eric's little sister was born, and how jealous he was. "Can you *please* have a baby?" he'd asked his mom again and again.

"You need a mom and a dad to have a baby," his mom had said. "And they have to want to have a baby together."

Gabe had known even then that that wasn't going to happen. His mom and dad were divorced—they had been divorced from the time he was a baby himself—and they wouldn't want to have another baby together, since they didn't even talk to each other except for a few words when one of them dropped him off with the other.

"You're enough for me, Gabe," his mother always told him. "I know you'd like a brother or sister, but I'm sorry. It's going to be just us." Sometimes she gave his head a squeeze and added, "You've got enough brains for two kids, anyway."

But Gabe kept hoping that his mom would surprise him. One time, last year, Gabe made the grave mistake of asking her, excitedly, if she was pregnant. That night, she took a big black garbage bag and cleared out the pantry of everything that tasted good, and Gabe had to rely on hanging out at friends' houses if he wanted to eat anything but leafy greens.

For some reason it never even occurred to him that his dad could be the one to get him a sibling, but that's what was happening. And the best part was that his new brother was already his age, because his dad was marrying a woman named Carla who also had a son who was ten, Zack. They lived 2,825 miles away in Los Angeles, California (a 6-hour plane ride or 43-hour drive or a 706-hour walk!). They were visiting New York now, and Gabe was going to meet them for the first time—*tomorrow!* But after they got married at the end of August, Carla and Zack were going to live in New York City with Gabe's dad, which meant that whenever Gabe went to visit his dad he'd also be visiting his brother.

Manhattan was close enough that Gabe could go visit on weekends. He and Zack could do all the fun city stuff together, like go to the Museum of Natural History, but he could also go home before he had to deal with what he imagined would be annoying things about having a brother 100 percent of the time, like fighting over using the computer or both needing the *P* volume of the encyclopedia at the same time. Everything about it was perfect, perfect, *perfect.*

As Gabe lay in bed—his homework done and on his desk even though he wasn't going to school tomorrow, and his duffel bag packed with clothes to spend two nights in the city—he thought about his new stepbrother. Would Zack look different in person than he did in pictures? Would he be taller or shorter than Gabe? (Gabe hoped they'd be the same.) Would he wear glasses for reading or distance? (Gabe's were for both.) Would he prefer chocolate or vanilla (Gabe liked vanilla), fiction or nonfiction (Gabe liked both equally), multiplication or division (Gabe preferred division, the longer the better)? *It doesn't matter,* Gabe decided. *I'll like him no matter what, because we're going to be brothers.*

Gabe fell asleep smiling. He was going to love his new brother. They were going to become best friends.

Chapter 2

ZACK

The next morning, Gabe stood in the middle of Penn Station, holding his duffel bag with his left hand and his mom's hand with his right. People rushed past them in every direction, even though it was 10:15, the middle of the morning—he'd be doing social studies if he was at school—and Gabe thought that these people should be at work. He scanned all the bodies and faces through his glasses, looking for his dad and wondering if each kid who passed could be Zack, even though that wouldn't make much sense.

"Here comes your dad," Gabe's mom said. She smiled and waved, and Gabe craned his head to look, but he was too short. His mom turned to Gabe. "Have fun, honey, and be nice to Carla and Zack."

"I will," Gabe promised. He was still trying to see who was coming, but a large woman with two suitcases had stopped right in front of him to examine a map, and he couldn't see anything around her.

"Only one soda with dinner, Gabe," his mom said, "and then water if you're still thirsty."

"Okay."

"And I don't know what Carla and Zack will be like, but—"

"Dad!" shouted Gabe. He dropped his duffel bag, let go of his mother's hand, and flung himself into his dad's waist.

"Gabe-o!"

"Where's Zack? And Carla?"

His dad put his hands on Gabe's shoulders and nodded his head toward the wall. "We'll go over there in a second. They're excited to meet you."

Gabe stood on his tiptoes and looked where his dad had nodded. He caught a glimpse of a woman with curly hair and a boy about his age who seemed to be wearing headphones.

"Just a minute," said his mom. She handed Gabe his duffel bag. "Be good," she said, and Gabe nodded, his eyes pointed in the direction of his new family members. "Remember about the soda, please," she said, "and listen to Dad. I'll meet you right here on Sunday at four, and we'll take the four-twelve back home together." She said that last one more to Gabe's dad than to Gabe, which was good because he wasn't really listening anyway.

"I got him," said his dad.

His mom nodded. "Congratulations on your engagement."

"Thanks." His dad patted Gabe on the head. "Say good-bye to your mom."

There was a lull in passersby, and Gabe was getting a pretty good look at Zack, who had spiky dark hair and was pressing buttons on a cell phone. It was hard to pull his focus away, but Gabe did. He gave his mom a hug and said, "Bye, Mom. See you on Sunday." Then he turned to his dad. "Let's go."

The two of them made their way through the crowd. Despite all his excitement and all the mental lists he'd compiled of things he could talk about with his new stepbrother, face to face with him, Gabe found himself suddenly nervous and speechless.

"Gabe," said his dad, "this is my soon-to-be new wife, Carla."

Carla extended her hand to shake Gabe's and gave him a smile that looked even nicer in person than it did in the pictures his dad had shown him—Gabe thought it could get her a role in a toothpaste commercial. She was also a lot taller and thinner than his own mom. *I couldn't make the mistake of thinking* she's *pregnant*, Gabe thought.

"Hello, Gabe!" said Carla. "I've been looking forward to meeting you!"

"Hi," Gabe said. He had mostly been looking forward to meeting Zack, but he didn't say so.

"This is Zack," Carla said.

Zack didn't look up from the phone he was using. "Hang on," he said.

"Zack," Carla said with a sigh. "Put your phone away and meet Gabe."

"Hang *on*," Zack said. He typed quickly into the phone's keypad, pressed send, and then closed up the phone and stuck it into his back pocket. Only then did he look up and seem to notice Gabe. "Hey."

"Hi," said Gabe.

"Sorry. I had to text back."

"That's your phone?" Gabe asked.

"Yeah. I know, it's kind of old. But the two-year contract is up in June, so I'll get a new one then. A couple of my friends have iPhones, but I don't really want one. I think they're overrated."

Gabe didn't know what to say, so he just said, "Yeah. Totally." A few kids in his class had their own cell phones, but his mom said he wasn't allowed to have one until high school, and that was fine with him. It wasn't like he talked to his friends on the phone. But now he wished he had one or at least knew about the technology in the latest models, so that he could have said an actual sentence to Zack. *Do people even say "totally"?* he thought. He wondered who Zack was text messaging now. Wouldn't everyone he knew be in school?

"What's your cell number?" Zack asked. "I'll missed-call you, and then you'll have mine."

"I don't have one," he admitted. There went his first opportunity to become best friends.

"Zack is only allowed to have one because there are no pay phones at the skate park," Carla said to Gabe. "And it's supposed to be for emergencies only," she added with a sigh that showed she had given up on Zack's following that rule.

"You two guys have a lot of things in common," said Gabe's dad cheerily. But before he could begin to say what, exactly, those things were, Carla tapped him on the shoulder and pointed to her watch. "Oh, right," said Gabe's dad. "We'd better get to the subway. Cake tasting at eleven."

Gabe's dad and Carla took off, hand in hand, down the crowded corridor. Zack started following them, and Gabe hurried to keep up with Zack.

"What's your bag from?" Zack asked.

Gabe glanced down at his duffel bag as he walked. He figured Zack was asking *where* he had gotten the bag because of the logo on the side, which had an open book and said, ALL-STAR READERS 2010. But instead of saying that his library gave it to him because he read eight books in the summer of 2010 (he actually read more than that, but you only needed to read eight to get the duffel bag), he told Zack what he used the bag for: "Swimming."

"Oh, cool," said Zack. "I like swimming, but I'm not on a team. I think swim practice is during the spring and the summer, and that's when I surf and go to the skate park, and this summer I'm going to take guitar lessons, too. And then in two summers, when I'm twelve, my mom will *finally* let me go to sleepaway camp, or at least that's what she says."

"I might go to sleepaway camp this summer," Gabe said. He decided, just for now, to leave out that the sleepaway camp was the Summer Center for Gifted Enrichment, and that the reason he wasn't sure yet was because he was waiting to find out how he scored on a special test to see if he got in.

"Dude, I am so jealous. You've *got* to go. Nothing is cooler than sleepaway camp. My friend went last summer and told me all these *awesome* stories about stuff he did with his camp friends."

Once again, Gabe found himself wondering how to respond to his brother. He had mentally compiled a whole list of funny stories to tell Zack—about the time his friend spilled lemonade on his pants right before his Math Fair presentation, and about how he and some students in Wings, his school's gifted program, made a fully functional robot and then had it roll into the teacher's lounge and say, "I come in peace"—but he had a feeling Zack wouldn't find any of them awesome. Gabe's stomach sank like it had the time he'd realized he'd written a whole book report without remembering to indent for new paragraphs. Like all his hard work was somehow wrong.

The four of them reached the subway entrance turnstiles, and Gabe's dad pulled out a MetroCard. "You remember how to do this, Gabe?" he asked.

Gabe nodded. He had only ridden the subway a few times before, and not since he last visited his dad a few months ago. But he didn't want Zack to think he knew nothing about *anything*.

"I'll go through first," said his dad, "and then pass my card back to you so you can use it too." He stepped up to the turnstile and swiped the card through quickly and smoothly. The little screen said GO $18.50 REMAINING, and his dad walked through. Then he passed the card back.

Gabe put down his duffel bag and swiped the card through, fast. He walked confidently forward, but the turnstile didn't move. He looked at the screen: It was blank.

"You had it upside down. Try again," Carla said gently, in the same tone his teacher would use when a student called a word an adverb when it was really an adjective.

Gabe looked at the MetroCard and felt his face turn red. The way he had swiped it, the black magnetic strip didn't even go through the reader. Thinking about how dumb it was that he could probably program that magnetic strip but could not run it through the machine properly, he swiped it again. Again, the turnstile arm wouldn't budge. PLEASE SWIPE AGAIN AT THIS TURNSTILE. He swiped again, as he was told. PLEASE SWIPE AGAIN AT THIS TURNSTILE.

"Do it a little slower," his dad replied.

Gabe could feel a line building up behind him and hear people sighing and shifting, impatient.

He swiped the card slowly. PLEASE SWIPE AGAIN AT THIS TURN-STILE. He did it once more, quicker this time, and finally, the screen read GO $16.25 REMAINING. Relieved, Gabe rushed through. "Here," he said to Zack, extending his dad's MetroCard over the turnstile.

"I've got my own," said Zack.

Gabe felt dumb again as he handed the card back to his dad and watched Zack walk easily through on his first swipe.

"Don't forget your bag, dear," Carla said. She held up Gabe's duffel from the other side of the turnstile.

"Oh, yeah. Whoops!" Gabe grabbed it quickly, so that Zack couldn't get a closer look at the logo. "Oh, man," he muttered.

"I know how you feel," Zack said as they all rushed to the subway platform and caught a train.

Gabe sat down next to his dad and Carla, but then he realized that Zack was going to stay standing, so he jumped back up.

"The other day, I went surfing with my dad in the morning," Zack continued, "and then we hit all this traffic on the way back from Malibu. So I was late for school, which normally would be great, but that day I missed an assembly that was actually really fun. And then we had a test in science that I totally forgot about," he said, "so I probably flunked it. And then I bought a *Diet* Coke instead of a regular one during lunch and didn't realize it until I already opened it and took a sip."

The subway started moving with a jolt, and Gabe grabbed on to the pole Zack was holding. He felt his heart beating faster and his blood running through his body, like he was coming alive with the train. Despite all that stuff about surfing and flunking tests, he had finally found something he and his brother had in common! "I *hate* Diet Coke," he said.

"It tastes like puke," said Zack.

Gabe grinned. He knew tons about puke. "Did you know that cows throw up, chew the vomit in their mouths, and then swallow it again?"

"That's nasty," Zack said excitedly.

The subway stopped, and a woman gave the two boys a look of disgust. "Thanks for ruining my appetite," she said before gathering her bags and walking off the train.

Gabe and Zack looked at each other with raised eyebrows. Then they cracked up.

"You're welcome!" Zack called after her.

Gabe glanced at his dad and Carla to see if they were paying attention. When he saw that they were involved in a conversation and there was no way he could get in trouble, he took his hand off the pole to cup his mouth and shout at the woman. "Flies eat their vomit too!"

Zack, still laughing, said, "Awesome."

Gabe stumbled backward as the train started moving again, but he got his footing before falling over. "Whee!" he said, which made Zack laugh harder.

"You're funny," Zack said, and Gabe was so happy, he thought he might burst right there on the subway. "Do those animals really eat their puke?"

"Yeah. I read about it in a book called *Grossology*, which is all gross science facts."

"That sounds like a cool book."

"It is! What's your favorite book? I have three: one for fiction, one for nonfiction, and one that's kind of in between. I also really like poems—" Gabe cut himself off when he noticed that Zack's expression had gone from *cool* to *boring* to *what's wrong with this guy?*

"Reading's boring," Zack said.

"Some books are boring," Gabe said, even though he could only think of two books he'd ever found boring, and one of those was his social studies textbook, which he thought was actually two fifths boring and three fifths interesting. "But some books are really good, like the *Grossology* one."

Zack shrugged. "So do you just, like, read all the time?" he asked.

"Oh, no," said Gabe. "I mean, I read sometimes, but not all the time."

Zack laughed. "There's this kid in my class who's so weird. One time, the teacher asked him what he did over the weekend, and he said his friend came over and they read books. Isn't that weird?"

Gabe crinkled his nose. "Really weird," he said, even though he and Ashley did that all the time, and even though last weekend he went to Eric's house just to help him solve all the logic problems in the brainteaser book he'd gotten for his birthday.

"Yeah, this kid's a real nerd," Zack said. "He goes to the gifted program and everything. And get this. He's on a math team." Zack looked at Gabe, waiting for him to laugh. "Math's not a sport! What do you do on a math team? Run around solving math problems?"

Gabe swallowed. "I know someone who's on a math team," he said with a shrug. "It doesn't seem that weird. And this guy's really cool."

Zack shook his head. "That's not possible. You can't be on a math team *and* be cool. Math team, gifted program, hanging out and reading—all those things automatically make you a geek."

Gabe took off his glasses, rubbed his eye with his palm, and put them back on. *I'm three-for-three*, he thought, instantly ashamed. He'd been called a geek before by some kids at school, but it never bothered him like this. He didn't really care what those people thought about him—he never even thought about it—because he had lots of friends. It wasn't like he was Paul Hefferberger, who smelled bad and kept a plastic lightsaber in his backpack, or Margie Smith, who never had anyone to talk to except the cat stickers on her lunchbox. But this wasn't just someone at school, this was his *new brother*. And he didn't want his own brother—the brother he'd been hoping for forever—thinking he was like Paul or Margie. He wanted Zack to like him. "So, being a geek is bad?" he asked.

Zack cracked up. "Dude, you are so funny! Get this. This kid in my class, he's such a nerd that he wants to keep going to school over the *summer*. So he's going to this special nerd camp. That must be the most boringest place in the world. A whole camp of geeks doing geeky things." He shook his head. "Just picture that!"

Gabe thought about his application to the Summer Center for Gifted Enrichment and how anxious he was to hear if he'd gotten in. "I can picture it," he said. Then, worried that the truth might somehow become visible—like his brain would start glowing through his skull or something—Gabe added, "Why would anyone want to *learn* things over the summer?"

"Because they're nerds," Zack said with a pitying but knowing shake of his head. "There better not be a lot of nerds at my new school here in New York. My mom made me go with her to look at it yesterday, and it seemed okay. I'm sure there'll be cool people for me to be friends with."

The subway pulled into the next station, and their parents stood up. Gabe's dad motioned with his head for Gabe and Zack to get off.

Zack patted Gabe on the shoulder. "I didn't really know if I wanted a stepbrother," he said, "but you're pretty cool."

Gabe tried to bite back the smile he felt breaking. He walked proudly through the station with his new family members. As they were climbing the stairs, he realized that the geeky logo on his duffel bag was facing out. He stopped, flipped the bag around, and then ran to catch up with Zack.

Chapter 3
EXTRA CAREFUL

Gabe worked hard throughout the day to keep Zack liking him. He agreed heartily when Zack pronounced the chocolate cake awesome and the carrot cake gross, even though he actually thought the carrot cake was pretty good and not at all carroty. He kept quiet when the baker's assistant became confused about how to multiply the cost of the slices by the number of guests, even though he had already figured out the total cost in his head.

He did slip up a few times, though. At dinner, when he saw that the five main-course options came with six choices of side dishes, he said, "Let's figure out how many different plates of food there could be! First we have to determine if it's a permutation or a combination."

Zack looked at him as if he had begun speaking German.

"Kidding!" Gabe said.

"Are you trying to make me think I'm at school?" Zack asked. "That's mean."

"Yep," said Gabe, thankful for an explanation. "I'm going to test you on it later. So, I hope you have a number two pencil. Or two number ones! Get it?"

Zack rolled his eyes, and Gabe stopped laughing immediately and said he had to go to the bathroom.

After that, he tried to be extra careful. Even though he had brought two books—a copy of his current favorite to give to Zack and one to read himself—he didn't take them out or even mention reading again. He felt eternally lucky that he didn't keep anything incriminating at his dad's apartment, except for a spare pair of glasses in a bathroom drawer that Zack would have no reason to open.

There was only one twin bed in Gabe's room, and it was covered with Zack's stuff. *This is going to be Zack's room after the wedding*, Gabe realized for the first time. He didn't feel happy or sad about that, just surprised that he hadn't put it together before.

"I'm going to get an extra bed in here soon," Gabe's dad explained, "so you'll both have a place to sleep when you visit, Gabe. But tonight one of you can sleep on the couch, or I've got sleeping bags if you'd prefer the floor."

"Shot floor," said Zack.

Glad he'd let Zack talk first—he might have said they'd flip for the bed, which apparently would have been the wrong answer—Gabe said, "I like the floor too."

And so they rolled out two sleeping bags side by side in the small room, neither of them sleeping in what both could call his own bed.

Zack went into the bathroom and came out wearing a pair of baggy gray pajama pants and no shirt. "My room in LA is bigger than this," he said as he slid into one of the sleeping bags. "Even my room at my dad's house is bigger, and that's smaller than my regular room. But I guess this place is okay."

"It's smaller than my room at home too," said Gabe. "Even though this building is twenty stories taller!"

Zack rolled his eyes, and Gabe rushed into the bathroom to avoid letting Zack see him turn red. Once there, he debated just wearing his T-shirt and underwear to sleep, but, pressing his luck, he reluctantly put on the pajamas he'd brought: a pair of pants and a shirt that had the entire human skeleton on them. Zack raised his eyebrows but didn't comment, and Gabe's clavicles sunk. At least Zack didn't know that he had brought these pajamas on purpose and had planned on performing an original song and dance that named all the bones. He made sure to be in his sleeping bag before his dad turned the lights out, so that Zack wouldn't see that the bones glowed in the dark.

"Good night, Skeleton Man," said Zack.

"Good night," said Gabe. He rolled onto his side to take off his glasses and place them on the floor without Zack seeing his glow-in-the-dark tibia. *Tomorrow*, he thought, *I won't make any more mistakes.*

Chapter 4
NERD CAMP

"We're dressed like penguins," said Gabe, looking at himself and Zack side by side in the tuxedo shop mirror. They were getting fitted for the tuxes they'd wear at the wedding at the end of the summer.

Zack started to waddle, but the man fitting his pant legs sighed loudly and gave him an exasperated look. "Sorry," Zack said.

Gabe pointed at Zack as though scolding him and tried not to laugh. He was getting fitted for a cummerbund, and if he laughed, he'd get a similar noise and look from the person measuring his waist.

"Penguins can fly, right?" said Zack.

Gabe didn't answer, even though he had done a whole unit on penguins in Wings. He thought he heard something. He closed his eyes. "Someone's cell phone is ringing," he said.

"I don't hear anything," said Zack.

"I have bat ears," Gabe said. "It's coming from your jacket, Dad."

"Go see who it is," his dad said from behind a dressing room curtain.

The measurer removed his hands from Gabe's waist, and Gabe ran to get the phone out of his dad's jacket pocket. "It's Mom," he said. "Can I answer it?"

"Sure."

"Hi, Mom!"

"Gabe, hi! Just the person I was calling to talk to. How's your weekend so far?"

"It's good. Dad and Zack and I are in the tuxedo shop, and I'm getting fitted for a cummerbund."

"All right," his mom said. "I'm sorry to bother you, honey, but you got some mail that I thought you'd want to hear about."

Gabe's eyes opened wide. "I did?"

"Yes."

His mom paused for suspense, and Gabe glanced at Zack. "Go ahead," he said.

"You got into the Summer Center for Gifted Enrichment!"

"I did?" Gabe repeated, his mouth spreading into a grin. "Yes!"

"Congratulations!" his mom said. "I saw a big envelope from Summer Center in the mailbox and opened it right away."

"So, I can really go?"

"Go where?" asked Zack.

"Of course," said Gabe's mom. "I'm looking through this, and it looks like you're going to have so much fun. I just don't know how you're going to pick which classes to take. They have everything. Poetry Writing, Chemistry, Rocket Science, Cryptology, Statistics, Geography, Shakespeare . . ."

"Go where?" Zack repeated.

"Sleepaway camp," Gabe said to Zack.

"You're really going to sleepaway camp!" Zack said. "That is awesome!"

"Not just any sleepaway camp," his mom said on the

phone. "Only the brightest of the brightest get to go. I'm very proud of you, Gabe."

Gabe blushed and prayed Zack couldn't hear her.

"I've always wanted to go to sleepaway camp," Zack said, clearly envious.

"So, what do you think you want to take?" his mom asked. "We should mail this back ASAP so you get your first choice. You have to take one math or science course and one humanities course."

"It'll be so hard to pick . . . ," Gabe said. *Only math* or *science?* he thought. *That's so unfair.*

"I'm going to text my mom," Zack said, taking out his cell phone. "Everyone gets to go to sleepaway camp but me. It's so unfair."

"Want me to read you all the options?" Gabe's mom asked. "Maybe Zack can help you decide."

Gabe looked over at Zack, who was typing on his phone so rapidly, it looked like he was playing himself in a heated round of thumb war. "I'll just look tomorrow," he said. "Bring the list so I can read it on the train."

"You got it," his mom replied. "Have fun at the engagement dinner, honey. I miss you."

"Miss you too, Mom. Bye." Gabe closed the phone and clicked the heels of his patent leather tuxedo shoes together. "I'm going to camp!"

Zack closed his phone. "You are the luckiest person in the world. You have to tell me everything about it, okay? We'll e-mail each other, or, if it's really, like, in the woods, then we can write actual letters."

Gabe was so happy, he worried he might pop the buttons on his sample tuxedo shirt. Not only did Zack think he was cool for going to camp, but he also wanted to keep in touch with him all summer, like they were real brothers.

"Is it a special swimming camp or something?"

"No," Gabe said. *It's nerd camp*, he thought. *Just like the one the kid you don't like is going to.*

"Just regular, then? That's cool."

The tuxedo attendant appeared from the back of the shop holding a cummerbund in each hand. "Back to the fitting area, please, boys."

As the attendant wrapped the black fabric around him, Gabe could see Zack looking at him in the mirror with unshakable respect and admiration, as if he had just single-handedly mapped the human genome—or had to take a leave of absence from school to become a professional ice cream taster. He was set.

The rest of the weekend with Zack went as well as Gabe had been imagining. The two of them got along as though they'd been friends their whole lives. *I'm not just a nerd*, Gabe told himself. *Zack wouldn't be friends with me if I was nothing but a nerd.*

With the badge of camp honor, Gabe no longer had to make sure everything he said or did would convince Zack that he was cool.

He just had to make sure Zack didn't find out the truth about Summer Center.

Chapter 5

THE MOVING OF CLOTHES-FOR-CAMP CITY

Gabe's clothes and camp supplies were laid out across his bed, grouped into categories and stacked in piles. It was a clothing city with T-shirt towers, notebook parks, and a sweatpants river running through the center. Gabe rolled a piece of paper and held it to his mouth like a megaphone. "Attention, residents of Clothes-for-Camp City. This is your mayor speaking. Prepare to be moved into a suitcase and taken to camp. I repeat, prepare to be moved into a suitcase. You will be transported to camp first thing in the morning."

"You ready?" his mom asked.

"Let's go," Gabe said.

She picked up the "Things to Take to Summer Center" list from Gabe's desk and began reading. "Ten T-shirts."

"Check." Gabe made his arm into a wrecking ball and rammed it through the T-shirt stack. He simulated the collapse noise. "Poooochchchch!"

His mom was not amused.

"What?" Gabe said as he gathered the T-shirts into a ball and dropped them into his suitcase. "The city has to come down to be transported. I warned the residents. They evacuated."

"I don't care about the residents. I care about the time I took folding all your clothes. How about you move everything neatly, not in a pile of rubble?"

Gabe sighed. "Okay."

"Okay. Six pairs of shorts."

Gabe slid one hand under the pile of shorts and another on top. He made a *beep-beep-beep* noise as he backed up the stack and lowered it into the suitcase. Then he came up and grinned. "Check."

His mom chuckled and rolled her eyes. "I'm going to miss you this summer," she said, "even if you are very silly."

"I'm going to miss you," Gabe said, "and Eric and Ashley and Zack."

"Well, let's get you all packed so you'll be done by the time Eric and Ashley get here." She glanced at the digital clock on Gabe's nightstand. It was right next to his pillow, but Gabe still needed to put on his glasses in bed to be able to read it. "If we go really quickly, you can even call Zack before they arrive."

They went back to the list. With each item and noise, the suitcase became fuller and fuller, until it was stuffed to the brim, clothes on the bottom and school supplies on top. It was so full that Gabe had to sit on it while his mom zipped it shut. "You can't open this until you get there," she said, "or we'll never get it closed again."

Into his backpack Gabe put his keep-in-touch kit, which included a folder full of FROM THE BUNK OF GABE PHILLIPS stationery that he'd printed, his address book, extra pencils, and two sheets of stamps. He added his spare pair of glasses and his goggles, which were also prescription (without them he could easily swim into the wall of the pool). Tomorrow morning he'd fill it up with the book from his nightstand and all of his bathroom stuff. He felt like he had packed up his whole life, and it was weird to think that when he unpacked all of it, it'd be to use it somewhere other than this room.

* * *

"Look at your suitcase," said Ashley when she and Eric arrived to have dessert and say good-bye. "It's bigger than Eric."

"Hey!" said Eric. He went and stood next to it. "I'm taller."

"Not by much," said Gabe.

"Just wait," said Eric. "I might grow so much while you guys are at camp that by the end of the summer, I'll be taller than both of you combined."

"Combined?" said Gabe. "You'd be a giant!"

Eric nodded. "That'll show you guys."

Ashley sat down on Gabe's suitcase. "So, Gabe is going to spend the summer doing math and writing poetry, I am going to day camp, and you are going to grow?"

"Grow a lot," said Eric. "Every time I write you, Gabe, I'll tell you how many inches I grew."

"I can't say for sure yet," said Gabe, "because I don't start my Logical Reasoning class till Monday, but I think that doubling your height in six weeks is not logical."

The phone rang, and Gabe's mom picked it up. She brought the phone to the door of Gabe's room. "Zack," she said.

Gabe took it. "Hey, Zack! What's up, man?"

Ashley sighed, and Eric rolled his eyes.

"You leave tomorrow, right?" said Zack.

"Yeah," Gabe said. "I can't wait. I just finished packing."

Eric tapped Gabe on the shoulder. "Did you already pack your Logical Reasoning book? I want to show it to Ashley."

Gabe put his finger to his lips and covered the mouthpiece of the phone. "Yeah, I packed it," he said.

"What'd you pack?" said Zack.

"Nothing," said Gabe. "Can I call you back later? Some of my friends are here."

"Oh," said Zack. "Don't worry about it, man. I just called to say good-bye. And remember, you have to write and tell me everything you do. Everything."

"I promise," said Gabe.

"Next year," said Zack, "we'll go to sleepaway camp together."

"Yeah! That'd be so cool."

"Okay. Bye, Gabe."

"Bye."

Gabe clicked the phone off and put it on his desk. Ashley and Eric were looking at him. "That was my stepbrother," he said.

"Duh," said Ashley. "He's not even your stepbrother yet, but you still talk about him every five minutes."

"And how cool he is," added Eric.

"That's because he is cool," said Gabe. "He's still so jealous that I get to go to sleepaway camp. I have to write and tell him everything."

"But he doesn't know that your camp is called the Summer Center for Gifted Enrichment," said Ashley.

"Well, no," said Gabe.

"And he doesn't know that everyone who goes there is really smart and you had to take a test to get in."

"No."

"And he doesn't know that when you're there, you'll be in school almost all the time. And that you're really excited about it."

Gabe sighed. "No, but come on. If he found out, he wouldn't like me."

Eric looked at Gabe over his glasses. "But you're going to write and tell him everything."

"It's camp," said Gabe, tapping his nose. "I'll do it somehow."

"Won't that be lying?" asked Ashley.

"No," Eric granted, "it'll just be a challenge."

"Yeah," said Gabe. He liked challenges.

Chapter 6
A LOGICAL CHALLENGE

That night, after he said good night to his mom but before he shut off his reading light, Gabe found himself thinking about Ashley and Eric and Zack and himself and camp. He thought about Eric's little sister and how she idolized Eric and copied everything he did. As glad as he was to be finally getting a brother, it would have been so much easier to have a *baby* brother, one who grew up admiring him and never made him wonder if he was a nerd.

Zack likes me so far, he reminded himself, *so I can't be a total geek, right? And I'm going to have tons of non-nerdy things to report from camp.* He wouldn't have to lie when he wrote to Zack; he'd just have to be careful. *And logical.*

He got out of bed and unzipped his backpack, which was on the floor next to his suitcase. He slid out what was going to be his Logical Reasoning notebook and opened it to the very last page. Since he hadn't started the class yet, he wasn't totally sure of how to do a logic proof, so he just did his best.

Problem: Am I a nerd who only has nerdy adventures?
Hypothesis: No.

To organize the proof, he made a chart and filled in the first row with evidence.

Proof:

THINGS I CAN TELL ZACK (I am not a nerd.)	THINGS I CAN'T TELL ZACK (I am a nerd.)
1. I'm going to sleepaway camp for six weeks!	1. It is the Summer Center for Gifted Enrichment.

That was a good, honest start. His summer was about to become one big logic problem. One awesome, fun, sleepaway, no-parents logic problem. He couldn't wait.

Chapter 7
WESLEY AND NIKHIL

Dear Eric,

Greetings from camp! I have only been here .6 days, but so far I LOVE IT!! I am writing to you FIRST, before my mom even, but my mom is still here. I'm in the library! We have a library here!

Here's what we've done the first day so far: We parked the car, and then my mom and me went to the camp office to check in. Someone gave us a map of the campground and told us how to get to my bunk, which is 2B. We went to the bunk and put down my suitcase and met my counselor. His name is David and he is in college. The bunk is a long rectangle, but it is divided up into small areas, kind of like rooms but without doors. There's just a space where a door would be. (See diagram A.) My bed is all the way in the last section, so it's kind of private. (See number 1 on diagram A.) It's not totally private because I share it with people named Wesley and Nikhil, but it's more private than the rest of the bunk because we only have three people instead of four. We came to check out the library. Now my mom has to go to a meeting for parents and I have to go to my bunk to unpack. Maybe I'll meet my bunkmates!

DIAGRAM A

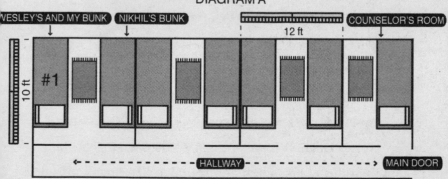

WESLEY'S AND MY BUNK   NIKHIL'S BUNK   12 ft   COUNSELOR'S ROOM

10 ft   #1

HALLWAY   MAIN DOOR

On one side of Gabe's suitcase was a duffel bag that could fit a person in it, and on the other side was a large trunk like a magician might have. *They belong to my bunkmates*, Gabe thought. He looked around. "Hello?" he said.

"Hello?" came a voice from the ceiling.

Gabe looked up. A thin boy with short black hair and black-rimmed glasses looked down from the top bunk bed he was sitting on. "I'm Wesley Fan," he said. "Are you Gabriel or Nikhil?"

"I'm Gabriel," said Gabe. "But call me Gabe."

"I'm Wesley," said Wesley.

"I know. You just said that."

"I was telling *him*." Wesley motioned with his head to the entryway, where there was a tall boy with dark hair that stuck straight up, making him look even taller. "Are you Nikhil?"

"Yes," said the boy. "I'm Nikhil."

"I'm Gabe," said Gabe.

"I'm Wesley," said Wesley.

The three of them looked at one another.

"Well, now we know one another's names," said Gabe.

Wesley laughed. It was a quick, spirited laugh that came out the sides of his mouth and sounded like breath mixed with spit. The noise made Gabe laugh, and then Nikhil joined in.

Instead of unpacking, which was what they were supposed to be doing, Gabe and Nikhil climbed up to the other top bunk, and the three of them started asking one another questions. Nikhil asked what classes they were taking, and they found out that they were in all different ones. Gabe asked their ages, and upon their discovering that they were all ten, he asked their birthdays.

"Did you know," said Nikhil, "you only need twenty-three people in a room to have a greater than fifty percent chance of finding two people with the same birthday?"

"No way," said Gabe.

"Yeah!" said Wesley. "We proved that in my math club. I can show you how."

"We're only three people," said Nikhil, "so the odds are a lot lower. But mine's January fifth."

"One-five?" Gabe said. "Mine's five-one! May first."

"All right!" said Nikhil. "We're inverse birthday buddies." They high-fived.

"My birthday's on Pi day," said Wesley.

Gabe gasped. "I love Pi day."

"What's Pi day?" asked Nikhil.

Gabe and Wesley gaped at each other through their glasses. "You've never heard of Pi day?" Gabe asked. "It's March fourteenth, so three-fourteen, like three point one-four, which is Pi. On my math team we celebrate it every year."

"We celebrate it in school," said Wesley. "We sit around in a circle and eat pies. Mmm."

Nikhil's jaw dropped in jealousy. He decided to tell his teachers about it next year, and he climbed down and wrote it in his notebook. "I don't *think* I'll forget," he explained, closing up the notebook, "but you know. Just to be safe."

"I love pie," said Wesley dreamily.

"Yeah, Pi is really useful in math," said Nikhil. "How many digits can you name after three point one-four?"

"I know ten," said Wesley.

Gabe's shoulders sunk. "I only know eight."

Nikhil stood up tall. "I know fourteen," he said proudly.

"Fourteen!" said Wesley.

"Since we taught you about Pi day," Gabe said, "can you teach us up to fourteen digits?"

"All right," said Nikhil. "I want to learn more anyway. I'll teach you guys to fourteen, and then we'll all learn more."

"Goal: We all know twenty digits of Pi by the end of camp," said Wesley.

Nikhil wrote GOALS on the top of a piece of looseleaf paper and the goal on the first line. Then he took out a roll of tape from the front pocket of his backpack and taped the paper to the wall.

Gabe felt his body tingle with what he realized was no longer nerves but excitement. He could totally spend six weeks with these two, no problem. They were having the sort of first meeting that he'd hoped to have with his stepbrother. Did that mean Zack would think they were nerds? Would he be able to write to him about Wesley and Nikhil at all?

"I took one of the top bunks," said Wesley. "Is that okay?"

Nikhil nodded enthusiastically. "I prefer the bottom. I know I probably wouldn't roll off—incidences of people rolling out of bed are actually quite low—but I prefer the bottom anyway. Just to be safe."

"I might roll off," Wesley said with a shrug. "I roll around a lot when I sleep."

Nikhil looked apprehensive, but he didn't say anything.

"Then I can pick top or bottom," said Gabe. "Where should I go?" he wondered aloud, tapping his nose.

"Well," said Nikhil, "if you don't really care either way, I'd prefer it if you slept on the bottom, below Wesley. I don't *think* my bed would collapse with someone sleeping on top of me—I'm sure they build these things using good materials and sound engineering—but you know. Just in case." He looked at Gabe with an expression that was trying very hard to be casual, but Gabe could see that he was really very concerned.

Gabe shrugged and jumped off the top of what was now Nikhil's bunk. "Okay," he said. "I'll take the other bottom."

"That means you don't have to solve this challenge," said Wesley from his perch atop Gabe's new bed. "Where am I going to put my book and my glasses and my tissues when I sleep?"

"On those posts?" Gabe suggested. He pointed to one of the wooden posts on a corner of the bed.

"I thought of that," said Wesley. "But I roll around, so it won't work. Look." He balanced a book on the post, then tapped underneath it with his hand. The book wobbled and fell down.

Nikhil shook his head nervously. "Yeah, don't put stuff there."

"You could hang a net from the ceiling," suggested Gabe. "And put stuff in there. That'd be cool."

"Oh, yeah," said Wesley thoughtfully. "But I don't have a net."

"And it could fall on you," said Nikhil.

"Wait!" said Wesley. "I got it." He shinnied down from the bed and began rummaging through the big duffel bag. He grinned and held up a tennis racket. He stood on the edge of Gabe's bed and wedged the handle of the racket underneath his mattress. Then he climbed back up and placed a book on the face of the racket. He moved his hands away slowly. "Ta da!" he said.

"Good thinking," said Gabe.

"Yeah, that's genius," said Nikhil.

Wesley held out his arms. "Thank you, thank you," he said. "I got into Smart Camp for a reason." He bowed deeply, then came up and hit his head on the ceiling.

Problem: Am I a nerd who only has nerdy adventures?

Hypothesis: No.

45

Proof:

THINGS I CAN TELL ZACK (I am not a nerd.)	THINGS I CAN'T TELL ZACK (I am a nerd.)
1. I'm going to sleepaway camp for six weeks!	1. It is the Summer Center for Gifted Enrichment.
2. My bunkmates are really cool, and we became friends right away!	2. They like learning digits of π.

Chapter 8
FIRST-NIGHT JITTERS

Dear Zack,

It is only the first night, but so far camp is awesome!!!
You would love it!! I have bunkmates named Wesley
and Nikhil, and we all get along great. Here's what
we did today after the parents left. We had pizza
for dinner, which was so good. And then we played
some games to get to know our bunkmates. Then we
toasted marshmallows! And then we had a HUGE
WATER-GUN FIGHT! It was extra fun because it
was already kind of dark out, so you could sneak up on

people. I got really soaked. Now I am back in my bunk. I have to go because it's almost lights out. You were right, camp is the best, and I am not feeling sad or missing home at all.

Gabe knew why it was called homesickness: He missed home so much that his stomach hurt. It wasn't that he didn't like camp; he did love it so far. He just wished he could teleport back to his own bed in his own room in his regular town for just a few minutes. He counted only eight times that he had spent nights away from his mom or dad, and all of those times were with his grandparents or with Eric, and his mom had been nearby.

His counselor said that the key to not feeling homesick was to not think about home. So Gabe sat up and looked through his backpack to make sure he had everything for his classes in the morning. He thought about how much fun the water-gun fight had been, and he mentally repeated Pi to the ninth digit in his head.

The counselor, David, shouted from his bed at the very front of the cabin: "Lights out in five minutes, guys."

"Five minutes," Gabe repeated.

"*T*-minus-five," said Wesley in a robotic voice.

"Mmm," muttered Nikhil nervously. "I still have five pages in this chapter. Good thing I put this over here"—he moved his flashlight from the floor to his bed—"just in case."

Gabe noticed that Nikhil was at the very end of his book. "You should have finished that before you came," he said, "so you didn't have to bring the book just to read the last chapter."

Nikhil's eyes kept moving over the page while he replied. "No, I haven't read this book yet." He turned the page and kept reading. "I like to read the last chapter first, just to make sure everything works out okay."

Gabe considered this. He thought reading the last chapter first would ruin the ending, but he guessed that for Nikhil that was the point. It was pretty brave of Nikhil to come to sleep-away camp at all; even Gabe was a little nervous about how the summer would work out, and he *liked* surprises.

So far, it seemed like one of the best things about camp would be a surprise: Color War. A few kids in his cabin had older siblings who'd gone to Summer Center, and it was all they could talk about. Just like field day at school, Color War split the entire camp into teams, and they competed in all sorts of physical and mental challenges. But there was a challenge even before Color War started: trying to figure out when Color War would break. It could happen at any moment and in any way. Last year, it even started the very first week of camp, and it had a circus theme, so it broke by the director of the camp riding in on an elephant!

"Hey, Nikhil," said Gabe casually, "when do you think Color War will break?"

Nikhil put his book facedown on his chest. "I've been thinking about it," he said. "And I think that if we compile a list of all the dates it's broken in the past, we can write a mathematical formula—you know, an algorithm—to figure out when it will break this year, within a few days, at least. I already recorded dates from the past three years. Victor is going to get me more from his older sister."

"I bet you're right," said Wesley. "I bet we can predict it."

"Cool," said Gabe. "Unless it breaks before we have time to get all the data. It could happen tonight!"

"That would be nuts," said Wesley excitedly. "I can't wait for Color War. I didn't know if I wanted to come here, but so far it's pretty awesome. And tomorrow is school. I can't wait to go to sleep so it'll come faster." He stared out the window by his bed, in the direction of the classrooms. "I really can't wait," he decided. "I'm going to go to sleep now." He took off his glasses and placed them on his floating tennis-racket nightstand.

"Okay. Good night," Gabe said, surprised. But then he was even more surprised when, as if a hypnotist had just snapped his fingers, Wesley was instantly out.

"Finished!" said Nikhil. He closed his book and placed it and the flashlight on the floor next to him.

"How was it?" asked Gabe.

"Really good. I'm definitely going to read it."

"Nikhil . . ."

"Yeah?"

Gabe felt a pang of homesickness and wanted to ask if Nikhil was feeling the same way. But if Nikhil wouldn't even read a book without knowing the story would end okay—a story that was completely made up—then he must have confidence that being at camp would end up all right, or he wouldn't be there. "Never mind," he said.

"Lights out in ten seconds!" their counselor shouted.

"You'd better get into bed," said Nikhil.

"On my way." Gabe jumped into bed and took off his glasses. The room dissolved into splotches of color. He turned his head to the blob that he knew was Nikhil. "Good night, Nikhil," he said.

"Good night, Gabe."

The bunk went black and, as if someone clicked a switch in his back, Gabe's supersenses kicked in. His eyes were so bad that if he held his hand in front of his face without his glasses on, he could only sort of make out the shape of a fuzzy bunny rabbit, and that was probably only because his brain knew it was a hand. But Gabe had a theory: At night, when he closed his eyes, his body could take all the energy it normally had to apply toward seeing and apply it to other things, which made his other senses superhero-like.

How different the sounds and smells here at camp were from what they were at home in his own bed. At home he would hear the muffled tapping of keys as his mom answered her e-mail, or the soft din of the news on TV. He'd hear the foggy drip of the coffeemaker and smell the fresh coffee. His mom liked her coffee cold, so she brewed a cup at night and put it in the refrigerator for the morning. Most people said, "Wake up and smell the coffee," but in his house the saying was "Go to sleep and smell the coffee." *No*, Gabe reminded himself, *don't think about home.*

He thought about the way Zack—who was going to be moving more than 2,000 miles at the end of the summer— just shrugged when he mentioned going to a new school and sleeping in a new, smaller room.

But thinking about Zack—and how different Gabe was from him—was no better than thinking about home right now. Gabe imagined an industrial digger scooping up his nervous thoughts like rubble and carrying them out of his brain. His mind cleared for rebuilding from scratch, he closed his eyes and let his body absorb the night.

He could smell the remnants of dinner and what might be the greasy start of tomorrow's breakfast. He could feel the moisture in the air that might bring rain. And he could hear the sounds of the entire campground and surrounding woods. At first all was quiet except for the low crackle of cicadas. But then from the open windows drifted chatter from outside, where the counselors were probably hanging out in a clearing. Some boys were whispering at the other end of the cabin, something about letting x represent the amount of candy they'd brought and y represent the number of days it had to last. In his corner of the cabin, both Wesley and Nikhil were breathing deeply and evenly. The bed creaked as Wesley rolled over to the wall.

"Mmm," mumbled Wesley. "Scuba mask."

Gabe put his hand over his mouth to keep from cracking up. *Scuba mask?* he thought. *What* was Wesley dreaming about?

Wesley flopped onto his back, making the bed shake. Gabe gripped the inside of his sleeping bag.

"Ha!" said Wesley. "Amoeba dance party!"

Gabe covered his face with his pillow to muffle his laughter. He didn't get to hear hysterical things like that at home! *What would an amoeba dance party look like?* he wondered. *They'd be really good at the limbo because they're so fluid!* Nikhil would probably be nervous about an amoeba dance party because if they danced too hard, some cytoplasm might spill and an amoeba could slip on it. He fell asleep imagining a line of protozoa shaking their single cells to the beat.

Chapter 9
AMANDA WISZNEWSKI

Dear Ashley,

It's 7:00 a.m., but I am awake already because I'm
so excited about my first real day of Summer Center!
Everyone will have to wake up soon, but I am writing
to you before the alarm goes off. Then we'll go to
breakfast. Actually, here's what I'll be doing every
day, starting today.

7:30 Wake up
8:00 Breakfast

8:45   Morning session. This is when I have Logical
       Reasoning.
11:30 Lunch
12:00 Recess
12:45 Afternoon session. This is when I have Poetry
       Writing.
3:30   Swimming in the lake
5:00   Free time
6:00   Dinner
6:45   Homework time
8:00   Snack and night activities
9:00   Back to bunks
10:00 Lights out
Repeat.

Gabe tilled his breakfast with his spoon. The man who had handed him the bowl said it was oatmeal, but Gabe instantly thought of the word "gruel." He could never really picture what gruel was when orphanages and step-parents served it in books, but examining the mound of murky brown goop on his tray, he felt a sudden empathy for orphans everywhere.

"Yesterday's food was so good," he said. "What happened?"

"The parents left," their counselor explained. "The food is only that good when parents are here."

"What state is this stuff in?" said Wesley. "Solid, liquid, or gas?"

Gabe poked the gruel with the tip of his finger and then held it up to his nose. "A little of all three, I think. It's a state that hasn't been recognized by science yet."

"What about plasma?" said Nikhil. "Plasma's kind of a fourth state."

Wesley snorted. "Our oatmeal is made of plasma!"

"I'm going to get some orange juice," said Nikhil. "I need something that's solid liquid." He chuckled. "I mean something that's *only* liquid. Something can't be solid *and* liquid at the same time, except right at its freezing point."

"Just don't get gas," said Wesley. "We have to sleep in your room."

Gabe cracked up, causing the scoop of oatmeal on his spoon to drop onto his tray. He picked it up with a napkin. When he saw how much it resembled something he could have just blown into the napkin from his nose, he felt even less inclined to eat.

Nikhil returned with a glass of orange juice and a cup full of lemon wedges. "Here," he said. "If you squeeze lemon juice on it, the acid in the juice will kill any bacteria."

Gabe and Wesley looked at each other, impressed. Nikhil blushed and shrugged.

Gabe finished squeezing his lemon and took his first bite of breakfast. "Mmm," he said. "Lemon-plasma oatmeal!" But it actually didn't taste half-bad, and Gabe was hungry. He began shoveling spoonfuls into his mouth.

It was only when he was walking into his Logical Reasoning classroom that he wondered if maybe he shouldn't have eaten so much. It was probably a combination of things that was making Gabe's stomach do somersaults: leftover homesickness, separation from his new and only friends at camp, first-day-of-school jitters . . . Add two bowlfuls of lemon-plasma oatmeal, and you had a recipe for queasiness.

"Are you going to puke?" asked a girl as they filed into the room.

Gabe shook his head. "I think I just ate a little too much oatmeal."

"A girl in my bunk puked last night," the girl bragged. "It was because she was feeling homesick. And did you hear that there was a boy who went home this morning? He cried until the counselors called his parents to pick him up."

"I just ate too much oatmeal," Gabe repeated. "I'm fine, though."

The girl wasn't convinced. "You look weird."

"You *are* weird," Gabe snapped.

The girl crossed her arms. "I was only saying you look weird because you look kind of sick. I don't think you look *weird*-weird. I actually kind of liked you, until you said that."

Big loss, Gabe thought. It wasn't like he was hoping the two of them would become best friends.

"Take a seat, please!" said their teacher, Miss Carey. "We've got lots of fun logical thinking to do this morning."

Gabe walked to the far end of the room before choosing a desk, hoping to sit as far from the annoying girl as possible. But she wandered along the U of seats as well and ended up right next to him. Gabe stared straight ahead, trying to ignore her presence.

She looked directly at him. "Fine," she said. "Apology accepted."

Gabe opened his mouth to say that he hadn't apologized, but he stopped himself. Miss Carey was in the front of the room. "Don't get too comfortable," she said. "These aren't your real seats."

Gabe smiled out of relief.

"In order to find your real seats," continued Miss Carey, "and to introduce you to logic, I've got a logic problem for you. You only need a pencil." She began passing out pieces of paper that had a list of clues on top. On the bottom was a chart that had each of the students' names running down the first column, and seat numbers, from the door to the windows, across the top. "Read the clues at the top and use the chart at the bottom to figure out who sits where. Then, when you think you know where your seat is, go sit in it. Then we'll see if you got it right."

"Is this a test?" asked a boy on the other side of the room.

"No," said Miss Carey, "it's not a test. It's just for fun."

"What if we can't solve it?" asked someone else.

"Just do the best you can."

Gabe took his copy of the problem from Miss Carey and looked at the first clue: "Amanda sits between two boys." Part of his jitters evaporated. This was fun! He *loved* problems like this. And the sooner he completed it, the sooner he could move away from the annoying girl next to him. He pulled out a freshly sharpened pencil and began working.

Amanda sits between *two boys*, he thought. *Since she's between two people, she's not at one of the ends.* He found Amanda on the list of students and put an X in the boxes for the first seat and last seat.

He skipped down the list of clues to one about him. "Gabriel's seat is closer to the windows than to the door."

That was easy. He located himself on the chart and X-ed the first half of the boxes, the ones that represented seats closer to the doors. He continued to work, reading a clue, thinking about what information it revealed, and filling in the chart. He made a mistake somewhere along the way—it didn't make sense for Michael to not have a seat—but he was able to go back and fix it. He was concentrating so hard that he barely registered the squeak of chairs along the floor as a few students figured out their spots and got up to move to them.

"Rose and Gabriel are as far apart as can be," he read. *I hope this annoying girl next to me is named Rose*, Gabe thought as he looked at the chart to solve the last of the clues. If he and Rose were as far apart as can be, that must mean they were sitting on the two ends of the U. And if his seat was closer to the windows than to the door, Rose must be at the seat closest to the door. And he must be closest to the windows, next to someone named . . . he checked his chart— Amanda. He only had to move one seat over, into the seat where the annoying girl (Rose, he'd convinced himself) was sitting right now. That meant he got to kick her out, which was an added bonus. He put down his pencil and looked up with satisfaction.

But before he could tap her and steal the seat, *she* poked *him* on the shoulder. "Thanks for keeping my seat warm," she said.

"What?" said Gabe.

"You're in my seat," she said.

"Aren't you all the way over there?" Gabe asked. He pointed to the seat by the door. As soon as he did, his hopes were dashed. In that seat was a girl with pigtails. She was wearing a T-shirt with a big picture of a rose on it, and the pencil case on her desk was plastered with roses.

The girl next to Gabe said, "Maybe you did it wrong. I'm Amanda. I'm right here next to—"

Gabe finished her sentence for her: "Me."

The girl broke into a smile. "Good thing I forgave you," she said. "We're meant to be."

And just like that, Gabe was back to feeling sick.

"Don't look," said Wesley. "There goes Amanda Wisznewski again."

Gabe put down his grilled cheese sandwich and rolled his eyes. "Why does she keep walking by here?"

"She must be really hungry," said Nikhil. "She's walked by so many times."

"But she doesn't even have to walk by our table to get more food," said Gabe. "She just keeps doing it to annoy me."

"Don't look," said Wesley. "She's walking back the other way."

"Let's talk about anything but Amanda Wisznewski," said Gabe.

"Okay," said Nikhil.

But for some reason, apart from Amanda Wisznewski there wasn't very much to talk about. The boys ate their lunch silently until a few minutes later, when Amanda walked by again and Wesley said, "I won't say who, but someone just walked by again."

Recess wasn't any better. Every time the boys turned around, Amanda and some girls from her bunk were right there. They tried to lose them by running in separate directions off the field, but when they met up in the woods, the girls were right near them, playing some sort of hopscotch game with rocks and logs.

Gabe wasn't even surprised when Amanda was in Poetry Writing as well. But the Poetry Writing teacher made up for that. Gabe knew he'd like Mr. Justice the minute he saw him. He was short and thin, with rimless glasses and thick dreadlocks that hung down to his elbows like the branches of a willow tree. From the way he kept the lights out in the classroom while he taught, to the low, sure pitch of his voice as he told the class he thought them mature enough to not need set rules, Mr. Justice created an atmosphere of such tranquility that Gabe thought he could forget about Amanda Wisznewski—if only she would let herself be forgotten.

When Mr. Justice asked them to get into pairs for a getting-to-know-each-other exercise, Amanda shouted out, "I pick Gabe Phillips!"

Mr. Justice saw Gabe take off his glasses and rub his

eyes, but he only raised his eyebrows and said, "Well, then."

Amanda pushed her desk close to Gabe's. "You're welcome," she said.

"What?"

"I said you're welcome. I knew you'd want to be my partner but would be too embarrassed to say it, so I said it."

Gabe wanted to close his eyes and ask her to repeat what she said, to make sure he'd heard it right. "Why do you think I wanted to be your partner?"

"Because I haven't been able to shake you all day."

Gabe blinked. "You think *I've* been following *you*?"

Amanda began counting on her fingers. "You sat next to me in Logical Reasoning, even before we had the assigned seats. Then you kept looking at me all through lunch. And talking about me—I heard you and your friends saying my name every single time I passed your table. Then you kept following me around during recess, even in the woods. And now you're in this class with me. It's kind of obvious."

Gabe didn't even know what to say.

"I forgive you, though, *again*." Amanda shrugged. "I've just accepted that we're meant to be."

Problem: Am I a nerd who only has nerdy adventures?

Hypothesis: No.

Proof:

THINGS I CAN TELL ZACK (I am not a nerd.)	THINGS I CAN'T TELL ZACK (I am a nerd.)
1. I'm going to sleepaway camp for six weeks!	1. It is the Summer Center for Gifted Enrichment.
2. My bunkmates are really cool, and we became friends right away!	2. They like learning digits of π.
3. The food is bad, just like at camps in ~~books and~~ movies!	3. We fixed it with lemon juice to kill the bacteria.
4. I'm being stalked by an annoying girl!	4. She is in my Logical Reasoning and Poetry Writing classes.

Chapter 10

KARAOKE SHOWDOWN

Zack—

Did you ever swim in a lake? It's not like the ocean, because the water isn't salty and there aren't really waves. Also, the bottom has mud instead of sand. It's kind of weird, but you get used to it. But one of the girl counselors dove down and scooped up mud and then rubbed it all over her body. She said it's good for your skin, and some other girls tried it. Gross!!

I think the best thing about camp so far is kayaking. They have kayaks that you can use during swim time. You sit in it and use a paddle and you can go all over and turn and stuff. It's SO FUN! Wesley tried it a few times, but he's so bad. He can't even paddle forward, and he even flipped over two times and the lifeguard had to come help him get out from underneath. Now he just sticks to swimming. I think the lifeguards are happy about that.

The worst thing about camp so far is Amanda Wisznewski.

"You know what's meant to be?" said Wesley. "Me and the play."

"What play?"

"The play that's happening this week during activity time. It's right here on the list. See? Playwriting."

It was the second Monday of camp, and even with time slowing down whenever Gabe waited for Amanda to disappear, the days were passing so quickly that Gabe worried camp would be over before he had a chance to try everything. Every afternoon during free time, the list of evening activities was thumbtacked to the post of the counselor's bed. You had until dinner to choose and sign up for what you wanted to do that night after homework. You could play sports, use the computers, make crafts, cook, watch movies—the list changed and grew, and everything on it sounded so fun that the boys often found themselves choosing by eenie meenie miney mo.

"I'll get the chart," Nikhil said. He walked to the back of the cabin and took the activities chart they'd made off the wall. It listed the day, the activity each of them had chosen, the type of activity, how fun it was on a scale of zero to five, and any additional comments. There was a row for each of them, plus a row for Amanda. The reasoning was that if they kept track of her choices, they could figure out what she'd choose next—and Gabe could avoid it. So far, that theory was failing miserably. The activity column had matching entries for Gabe and Amanda four out of the six days.

"I think we're all due for a sport tonight," Nikhil said after reviewing the chart. "Except maybe you, Gabe, since you played Spud on Thursday. But you gave it a four point five, so maybe you want to do another one anyway."

"I'm doing the play," said Wesley. "I'm going to star in it."

"You like being up there in front of people?" asked Nikhil.

"Yeah," said Wesley. "I wanted to go to acting camp, but

when I got into Summer Center, my parents said I had to come here."

"This wasn't your first choice?" asked Gabe. He put a mental tick in his non-nerdy column—Wesley wasn't a complete nerd. Unless acting was nerdy. Zack probably thought so.

Wesley shrugged and shook his head. "My mom and dad think school is the most important thing. Plays are just for fun. That's why I'm here." He brightened. "But they're not here. So I'm doing the play." He rubbed his hands together sinisterly.

"The play is every day for a whole week, right?" asked Nikhil. "If you don't like it, you're stuck."

"I'll like it," said Wesley. "I'm going to be the lead."

"How do you know you'll get the lead?" asked Gabe.

Wesley smiled, as if he'd been waiting for this question all day. "This week, you sign up to *write* the play. Then, next week, you sign up to be in it. So, I've got a foolproof plan. I'm going to do both. And I'm going to write the lead part so that it's perfect for me."

Gabe and Nikhil looked at each other and nodded. That was a smart plan.

Nikhil said, "Gabe, maybe you should do the play. If

Amanda doesn't do it, you'd have two whole weeks without her, guaranteed!"

Gabe considered this. "But if she does do it, I'll have two weeks *with* her, guaranteed."

Nikhil moved his head from side to side. "You're right," he decided. "It's not worth the risk."

Gabe took the chart from Nikhil and looked at the list on their counselor's bedpost. The choices were all good, as usual. There were a few options for sports, but he was pretty tired from kayaking during swim time. Since Nikhil was going to do one of those and Wesley was going to do the play, that meant Gabe was on his own. Silent reading called out to him like it did every time it was on the list. But then, like every time it was on the list, he reminded himself that he could read before lights out, and if he did it during activity time, he might be missing out on some of the more original options. Last night he'd thought the same thing and then ended up choosing baking cookies. Unfortunately, so did Amanda, so he spent the hour defending his ratio of chocolate chips to dough and trying to keep her grubby fingers out of his mixing bowl.

What *wouldn't* Amanda pick tonight? Her row of the chart was completely illogical; there was no pattern to it at all. Sometimes she picked completely girly things, but other times she'd be the only girl in the group. On Tuesday she made friendship bracelets, but then on Thursday, while most of her bunkmates were having a dance party, she was a running back on Gabe's flag football team.

What will Amanda not do? Gabe wondered, tapping his nose. But then he took it one step further. *She probably assumes I'll pick something she would not want to do*, Gabe reasoned. *So, I should pick something she normally* would *do.* He made a mental note to ask Miss Carey what that sort of reasoning is called.

"What's karaoke?" he said.

"Karaoke!" said Nikhil. "I studied that word for the spelling bee. The language of origin is Japanese, and it means musical accompaniment without vocals."

"Singing," Wesley translated. "I bet it's all girls."

"That's what I thought," said Gabe. "I think that's something Amanda would do but would think I wouldn't do."

Nikhil moved his eyes back and forth, processing each piece of that statement as if it were a volley in a tennis match. "I concur," he concluded.

"I concur squared," said Wesley.

"Perfect," said Gabe. "I'm doing it."

And that was how Gabe ended up in a room with Amanda, eight other girls, and an hour of girl singers' greatest hits.

He made a new mental note to tell Miss Carey that that sort of reasoning totally backfired.

"I didn't know you like singing," Amanda said while Jenny Chin and Vidya Gupta sang/screamed, "Girls just wanna have fun!"

"I don't," Gabe grumbled.

"Then why did you pick karaoke?"

"It's a long story."

"Is it because you thought I would do it?"

Sort of, Gabe thought. Then he had an idea. "Yep," he said. "What activity are you going to do tomorrow? Tell me so I won't have to guess."

But Amanda managed to turn that around too. She patted him on the shoulder. "I don't know what the choices will be tomorrow, but if it's meant to be, then we'll end up together."

Jenny and Vidya finished their song, and they curtsied while everyone clapped.

"Do you want to sing?" the counselor asked Gabe.

He shrugged. He wanted to be playing kickball with Nikhil. Even the play would be more fun.

"There are a lot of good choices," the counselor said. "I'll bring you the song list."

Gabe shrugged again.

"Don't be embarrassed," Amanda said knowingly. "It's okay if you're not that good."

Before Gabe could respond, Amanda took to the stage for her solo.

Not that good, Gabe thought. He took the list of songs from the counselor and began flipping through, determined to find a masterpiece with which he could wow the group.

The intro music for Amanda's song ended, and she began belting out the lyrics with gusto. "FIFty NIFty United States!" she sang.

Gabe looked up from the song list and wrinkled his forehead. *They have that song in here?* he thought.

"Alabama, Alaska . . ."

This was Amanda's big solo? Singing all the states in alphabetical order?

"Florida, Georgia," Amanda fluttered in a squeaky soprano.

Gabe's expression changed into a wry smile. He looked back at the long song list, this time with purpose. *Yes*, he thought when he found the song he was looking for. *I can't believe they have it.* This would show her, and it would blow everyone away: double whammy.

He copied down the title on a piece of paper and handed it to the counselor. She took a look at it and nodded, visibly impressed. Then she put her finger to her lips and stuck Gabe's song on top of the pile instead of at the bottom. "You're up next," she mouthed.

Gabe interlaced his fingers and pushed his hands away from him. He took a few deep breaths and jiggled his body, loosening up the way he would before a swim meet. He wished his bunkmates were there to watch this, and Eric and Ashley from home. The only person he was glad wasn't there was Zack—he had a feeling his song would ace Zack's nerd test. But he wasn't about to pass on an opportunity to one-up Amanda.

Amanda finished with one hand holding the microphone sideways by her mouth and the other hand up in the air, fingers wiggling. "Wyoooooming!"

Gabe thought there was no need for that extra-long "Wyoming," but he applauded politely while the rest of the audience whooped and cheered. Amanda bowed and remained on the stage, smiling proudly.

"Next up," announced the counselor, "Gabe Phillips, singing 'The Countries of the World.'"

Game time.

Gabe hopped up onto the stage and took the mic out of Amanda's hand. He didn't meet Amanda's judging eye; rather, he looked past her and tried his hardest to appear casual, as if he had just chosen a song at random and was only going to sing it in the shower.

"Testing," he said into the mic. The counselor gave him a thumbs-up. Her eyes asked, *Are you ready?* He returned it. *Am I ever.*

The music started up. The screen of the karaoke machine showed the name of the song in front of a map of the world. Then the map broke into a montage of images from around the world, and the first line of the song—the first five countries of the world, alphabetically—appeared on the bottom in white. The words began turning yellow, and Gabe sang out loudly and clearly: "Afghanistan, Albania, Algeria . . ."

The girls in the corner put down the song list and turned to the stage, curious. The counselor started clapping.

Amanda watched with her arms crossed and her eyes narrow.

"Does this name *every* country?" a girl asked.

"Yeah," said another. "I've heard it before."

"He knows them all?" the first girl asked.

Gabe began to dance around. He kicked and crossed his feet, and waved around the hand that wasn't holding the mic. "Chad, Chile, China . . ."

The girls began laughing and clapping. The counselor whistled. Gabe was getting into it.

"Wow," said Jenny Chin to Amanda. "He's good. I can only name the countries of North America and Europe."

"Yeah," said Vidya. "Africa is hard."

Amanda said loudly, "He probably doesn't know them all. He has the words right there."

Gabe heard her during the musical interlude between Fiji and Finland. *I have the words right here?* he challenged Amanda silently. He looked straight at her. Then he turned around so he faced the wall. Just to ensure that she didn't think he could see a reflection of the screen somehow, he took off his glasses and held them above his head. "Germany, Ghana, Greece . . . ," he sang.

The group of girls in the corner jumped to their feet and shrieked their approval.

Gabe put his glasses back on and began doing jumping jacks like they were a dance. Since he was still facing the wall, he assumed the rise in applause was for his perfect pronunciation of Kyrgyzstan through Liechtenstein. He stopped singing when he heard another voice join his on Namibia.

He whirled around, almost tripping on the microphone cord.

"Nicaragua, Niger, Nigeria, North Korea!" sang Amanda.

Gabe's jaw dropped open. Who said he wanted to do a duet? He sang louder: "Paraguay, Peru, Philippiiiiiines."

Amanda matched his volume. "Poland, Portugal."

Gabe covered his eyes with his arm. "Qatar, Romania."

Amanda did the same. "Russia, Rwanda."

The two of them went on like that, alternating every line, while the crowd roared. With each increase in volume the accuracy of the notes went down, but this was no longer about musical quality. It was a full-on alphabetical geography battle, and the audience was eating it up.

"United Kingdom," shouted Gabe.

"United States," answered Amanda.

"Uruguay!"

"Uzbekistan!"

"VANUATU!"

"VENEZUELA!"

They finished: "Vietnam, Yemen, Zambia, ZIMBAAAAA-BWEEE!"

Everyone broke into wild applause.

"Take a bow!" the counselor called.

Gabe bowed deeply. His glasses slid down his sweaty nose, and he had to reach up and stop them from falling.

Amanda held up both her hands and waved to the crowd as though she were an Olympic figure skater who had just completed a perfect routine.

"I was going to sing that next," Amanda said to Gabe as the two of them stepped off the stage. "But don't worry. I forgive you for stealing it."

Back in the bunk, Gabe told Wesley and Nikhil the story of how Amanda barged in on his countries song but he took her down in battle. They thought the story was so good that they made him repeat it for some other boys, and then some more. By the ten-minutes-to-lights-out warning, all the boys, plus their counselor and the counselor from the next bunk over, were crowded into Gabe's section. They sat on the beds, sprawled across the floor, and hung from the bedposts in order to watch Gabe reenact the battle, complete with the entire countries song, dance moves, a pencil-case microphone, and a falsetto Amanda voice.

It was a story that would go down in camp history. But when Gabe settled into his bed and took out his notepad before lights out, he realized that, once again, it wasn't one that he could tell to Zack. Despite all the cool stuff that was filling up the first column, there were just as many condemning things filling up the second.

Just imagine if Zack—Zack, who took guitar lessons and had his own surfboard—had seen the karaoke contest. Gabe could picture his look of pure embarrassment—no, utter *repulsion* at this geeky freak who was going to become his stepbrother.

He took off his glasses, and the real world dissolved into fuzz. But an image of his world as Zack must see it came in crystal clear, and it was humiliating. *I'm surrounded by nerds*, Gabe thought.

Problem: Am I a nerd who only has nerdy adventures?

Hypothesis: No.

Proof:

THINGS I CAN TELL ZACK (I am not a nerd.)	THINGS I CAN'T TELL ZACK (I am a nerd.)
1. I'm going to sleepaway camp for six weeks!	1. It is the Summer Center for Gifted Enrichment.
2. My bunkmates are really cool, and we became friends right away!	2. They like learning digits of π.
3. The food is bad, just like at camps in ~~books and~~ movies!	3. We fixed it with lemon juice to kill the bacteria.
4. I'm being stalked by an annoying girl!	4. She is in my Logical Reasoning and Poetry Writing classes.
5. I creamed Amanda in a sing-off!	5. We sang all the countries of the world.

Chapter 11

ARCH RIVALS

Gabe,

Here is a letter from ME (Eric) and me (Ashley)! We are alternating sentences. We are at Eric's house and we had breakfast for dinner. My sister says hi and I can't believe I had to waste my sentence on that.

We went to the first summer reading party tonight at the library. It was fun and we missed you and the librarian said we could take a summer reading poster for you because she's sure you've read three books already so we will mail it with this letter and also did Color War break yet?

Now Eric is just trying to write longer sentences than me and that is not fair or grammatical so I am going to write a really long run-on sentence even if it doesn't say anything so blah blah blah bl Ashley stop it, sorry Gabe, before this gets out of control I will tell you that I grew half an inch! He looks the same to me!!

Okay, I am going to just write you my own letter so bye (for now), Gabe.

Folded up, the summer reading poster didn't look like much, but once Gabe started unfolding it, it got bigger and bigger until it was almost as wide as his bed. The library theme this summer must have been music, because the poster said READING ROCKS and had a picture of books in the shape of a guitar.

"Whoa," said Nikhil, looking at the poster, which now covered Gabe's sleeping bag. "Cool!"

"That's so cool," said Wesley. "We have to put it up on the wall."

The Gabe part of Gabe wanted to agree, but ever since the night of his karaoke routine, he was starting to look at things the way Zack might look at them. And reading was definitely not cool. Reading, in fact, was the very first strike Zack had discovered against him. Gabe didn't think he needed to stop reading—he would never do that—but he didn't think he needed to advertise his love of it, either.

"Yeah!" said Nikhil. "We should put it up next to the reading chart. It'll probably fit, but I'll measure. Just to be safe."

The reading chart was where the three of them recorded which books they'd read, with columns for title, author, who read it, score out of ten, short summary, and favorite quotes. *Nerdy*, Gabe thought. Above the reading chart, on a long scroll, stretched Pi to the twentieth digit. *Double nerdy*, Gabe thought. Wesley had 3-D geometric shapes hanging like mobiles by his bed, Nikhil had a large periodic table along the length of his, and Gabe's bedposts were covered with photocopies of his favorite poems. *Nerd-a-palooza*, Gabe thought; he could just hear Zack's voice.

"I don't know if we should hang that up," Gabe said, his head tilted and his nose scrunched.

"It'll fit," said Nikhil. He was still holding his ruler.

"Okay," Gabe said, trying to be casual. "But do you ever wonder if maybe—I don't know—we could put different stuff on our walls?"

"You mean like Fun-Tak instead of tape?" said Wesley.

"No, like different kinds of posters that don't have to do with school or learning. Things that *normal* people would find cool, so our bunk isn't so geeky all the time." Gabe regretted the words the moment he finished saying them. The silence that followed made him wish words, like water, could evaporate and disappear.

David poked his head in from the doorway. "Lights out in ten, guys. Hurry up and hit the bathrooms before it's too late."

Gabe grabbed his toothbrush and rushed to the bathroom, leaving his words behind to hang in the air. He brushed his teeth inside one of the toilet stalls, and he didn't come out until he was sure the bathroom was empty. By the time he got back to the bunk, the lights were out, and he slid quietly into his sleeping bag, praying his bunkmates were still silent because they were asleep.

Gabe woke up prepared to say he wanted to hang the READING ROCKS poster after all, but there was no one to say it to. Nikhil's bed was made up neatly, and Wesley's sleeping bag was in a heap on his mattress. He got ready and walked to breakfast alone, hanging behind the rest of the kids in his cabin. He had a stomachache, but it wasn't from homesickness or eating too much oatmeal. He was pushing some scrambled eggs around with his fork when Wesley and Nikhil came rushing to sit on either side of him. They were out of breath, and Nikhil was holding a stack of papers.

"Gabe, just wait'll you see what we got!" said Wesley.

"David said we could go to the computer lab before breakfast," Nikhil explained. "So we brainstormed what would be cool to put up, like you said."

Wesley made a noise like a clap of thunder and moved his hands like a bolt of lightning was hitting his brain. "We decided on music and sports," he said.

Gabe felt his mouth spreading into a grin. The guilty feeling was replaced by a warm, tingly one, a genuine love of his bunkmates. This was going to be a step in the right direction, he just knew it. "Let's see!"

"Music," said Nikhil. "We got a guitar—one without books on it." He held up that picture, then the next one. "And clip art of some music notes." His voice trailed up at the end as if inviting Gabe's approval. When he didn't get it, he kept going. "Treble clef . . . and bass clef—we didn't know which you like better, so we got both. Just to be safe."

"We can put them on opposite sides of the room," said Wesley, "like they're enemies. And—show him the other one, Nikhil—a picture of Beethoven, who's the awesomest composer ever."

Gabe's spirits were sinking. They were trying, all right, but these guys just didn't get it. "What'd you get for sports?" he asked.

"A football." Wesley held up an enlarged clip-art image of a football.

Gabe tried to smile.

"The Olympic rings," Wesley continued, showing it off. "And the official rules of badminton!" Beaming, he showcased three pages of words. "I can't *wait* to read these."

"I wanted to put up the rules of Ping-Pong," said Nikhil.

"But Wesley thought we should only have one racket sport."

"Actually," said Wesley, shoveling some eggs into his mouth, "if we do both, we can put them on opposite sides of the room, next to the other archrivals"—he swallowed—"treble clef and bass clef."

"Yeah!" said Nikhil. "I like treble better."

"Bass rules!" shouted Wesley.

"No way. Treble clef forever!"

"That's it. Prepare to die!"

Gabe leaned out of the way as the two of them began swordfighting with their knives. They kept going until a passing counselor made them stop, even after Nikhil offered to wrap both knives in napkins, to be safe.

Gabe spent the day convincing himself that these posters were better than nothing—and they were definitely better than losing his bunkmates as friends, like he'd feared this morning. They hung them up that night before lights out. Gabe dispensed the tape, which required the least amount of involvement, while Nikhil took care of measuring and leveling and Wesley provided the sound track of an original bunkredecorating theme song.

"This looks awesome," said Nikhil when they were done.

"There are a lot of new things," said Gabe, not wanting to lie. "And the badminton rules are very interesting," he added. That was also true.

"Good night, Beethoven," Nikhil said as he climbed into bed. "And Wesley and Gabe and football and Olympic rings."

Gabe couldn't help but laugh. "You forgot about the treble clef."

"Team Bass!" Wesley shouted.

Problem: Am I a nerd who only has nerdy adventures?
Hypothesis: No.

Proof:

THINGS I CAN TELL ZACK (I am not a nerd.)	THINGS I CAN'T TELL ZACK (I am a nerd.)
1. I'm going to sleepaway camp for six weeks!	1. It is the Summer Center for Gifted Enrichment.
2. My bunkmates are really cool, and we became friends right away!	2. They like learning digits of π.

THINGS I CAN TELL ZACK (I am not a nerd.)	THINGS I CAN'T TELL ZACK (I am a nerd.)
3. The food is bad, just like at camps in ~~books and~~ movies!	3. We fixed it with lemon juice to kill the bacteria.
4. I'm being stalked by an annoying girl!	4. She is in my Logical Reasoning and Poetry Writing classes.
5. I creamed Amanda in a sing-off!	5. We sang all the countries of the world.
6. We put music and sports pictures on our walls.	6. They are of Beethoven and the rules of badminton.

Chapter 12

SLEEPING GENIUS

Most nights, Gabe was so exhausted from the day that he conked out as soon as the bunk went dark. But tonight he lay awake for a long time thinking about the new decorations. Treble and bass clef weren't exactly what Zack would think of when he thought about music. And badminton, interesting as its rules were, wasn't exactly the world's coolest sport. All in all, the room was probably just as nerdy as it'd been before.

Trying to forget about it, Gabe closed his eyes and listened. The air was thick like pea soup, and though Gabe could make out some sounds from outside, they were muffled. It was as if the cicadas were buzzing from inside a bowl of Jell-O.

"What's that?" said Wesley suddenly.

Gabe startled. He lifted his head and looked around, but he couldn't figure out what Wesley was asking about.

"Hel-*lo*," Wesley intoned. Then he added forcefully, "Mousepad."

Gabe almost choked on his laughter. Wesley was most definitely asleep. He often talked in his sleep—but could he listen, too? "What about mousepad?" Gabe said.

Wesley sighed. "I don't know. Just mousepad."

Gabe smiled. "Okay."

Wesley rolled over so that his whole body was up against the wall. He didn't say anything for a few seconds, and Gabe's shoulders sank. He took off his glasses and flopped over onto his stomach. He tried counting sheep, first in multiples of two, then in multiples of three.

"Oh," said Wesley suddenly. "The Pythagorean theorem."

Gabe opened his eyes into his pillow. He turned onto his side so that he could hear better.

"*X* equals seventy!" said Wesley.

Was he solving math problems? "What's four times five?" Gabe tried.

"No," said Wesley with a laugh. "Number fifteen is hard."

Gabe covered his snicker with his hand. Clearly, Wesley only wanted to solve problems like number fifteen, hard ones that required the Pythagorean theorem.

Wesley mumbled something Gabe couldn't make out. But then he spoke clearly once more. "The square root of sixty-five."

He said it with such certainty that Gabe knew it was important. He put his glasses back on and fumbled for a pencil and paper. It was difficult to write in the dark, but Gabe did the best he could. $X = 70$, #15, $\sqrt{65}$, he scribbled.

"Got it," he said to Wesley.

"Toyota Corolla," Wesley replied with a romantic sigh.

Gabe was groggy when the wake-up siren sounded in the morning, but he jolted to life when he remembered what had happened the night before.

"Wesley!" he said. He jumped out of bed and poked Wesley's knotted sleeping bag, trying to find his body.

"Good morning to you, too," said Nikhil, who was folding his sleeping bag neatly.

"Morning, Nikhil," Gabe said quickly. "Wait'll you hear about Wesley. Wesley!"

Wesley opened his eyes slowly and tried to stretch, but his sleeping bag was so tightly wound from him rolling around all night that he couldn't. "Good morning," he said through a huge yawn. "Are you ready?"

"I'll do it," said Nikhil. He clicked the side button on his watch to select the stopwatch mode. His finger poised over the start button, he said, "Ready . . . set . . . GO."

Wesley began to twist around like a worm trapped in a spiderweb. He kicked his legs, which made the bottom mass of the bag wave up and down. "How long so far?" Wesley asked.

"Six seconds," said Nikhil. "Seven. Eight . . ."

Wesley rolled over once, then again in the same direction. The bag was now unraveled at the bottom, but his arms were still trapped at the top. "Bottom's up!" Wesley called. He scooted on his back until his legs were hanging off the bed.

Gabe took a step back, and Nikhil closed his eyes but kept his finger on the stop button.

"Land ho!" Wesley slid down off the top bunk and squirmed like crazy in the air. He landed in a heap on the floor.

Gabe waited. Nikhil opened one eye.

Wesley jumped up, throwing his arms in the air and leaving the sleeping bag limp on the floor. "Ta da! How long?"

Nikhil pressed stop. "Sixteen point four," he reported.

"You could be an escape artist like Houdini," said Gabe. "You could get out of a straightjacket underwater."

"No offense," said Nikhil. "But I don't think Houdini would take sixteen seconds to get out of a sleeping bag."

"He would if he rolled around as much as Wesley in his sleep."

Nikhil walked to the graph on the wall and found that day's date with his finger. His bunkmates watched as he slid his finger up to halfway between sixteen and seventeen seconds and put a dot. He took a step back and looked at the graph. "Not as fast as yesterday, but still not as slow as July seventh."

"I'll never be as slow as July seventh. It'll go down in history."

On their graph, the line rose steeply to a dot at forty-five seconds, the time it had taken Wesley to get free from his sleeping bag the morning of July 7. It made the graph look like a heart monitor with only one spike of life.

Wesley pulled some wrinkled clothes out of his duffel

bag. "I've got to hurry," he said. "I have a couple of geometry problems to finish before breakfast."

Gabe clapped his hands once. "Were you thinking about your homework last night?"

"Yeah," said Wesley. "I had a dream that I was in Shapeland." He shuddered and shook his head.

The other two looked at each other. Shapeland must not have been a pleasant place.

"Well," said Gabe. "I bet the answer to one of your homework problems is x equals seventy."

Nikhil and Wesley looked at each other, waiting for an explanation. Nikhil moved his finger around his ear.

"Just check it," said Gabe, smiling. "You use the Pythagorean theorem."

Wesley took out his geometry book and unfolded the piece of paper that he'd stuck in between the homework pages. He did a few calculations. When he got the answer, he paused for a second before looking up with suspicion. "How'd you know?"

Gabe's eyes became rounder. "No way. It's really x equals seventy?" His mouth fell open. This was certainly nerdy, but it was so unbelievable that Gabe couldn't be anything but amazed.

"Did you do Wesley's homework after lights out?" asked Nikhil.

"No," Gabe explained. "Wesley did it in his sleep!"

He told them what he heard, and Wesley plugged "√65" into problem number fifteen, which also ended up being right. Nikhil was in awe, but Wesley claimed that Gabe had waited until he'd fallen asleep, taken out his math book, and done the problems by flashlight.

"I didn't," Gabe insisted. "How would I even know what problems to do or how to use the Pythagorean theorem? I just heard you say it before I fell asleep. You also said 'Toyota Corolla.'"

Wesley gasped. "I was driving a Toyota Corolla in Shapeland," he remembered. "Those problems were *so* hard. I'm a genius at night!"

"Did I say anything?" Nikhil asked Gabe hopefully.

"No," said Gabe, but Nikhil looked so disappointed that he added, "but maybe you did after I fell asleep."

"We should set up a recording system for after lights out," said Wesley. "Tonight I might solve the mystery of life."

"What's the mystery of life?" asked Nikhil.

"I don't know," said Wesley. "That's why we should record what I say."

Problem: Am I a nerd who only has nerdy adventures?

Hypothesis: No.

Proof:

THINGS I CAN TELL ZACK (I am not a nerd.)	THINGS I CAN'T TELL ZACK (I am a nerd.)
1. I'm going to sleepaway camp for six weeks!	1. It is the Summer Center for Gifted Enrichment.
2. My bunkmates are really cool, and we became friends right away!	2. They like learning digits of π.
3. The food is bad, just like at camps in ~~books and~~ movies!	3. We fixed it with lemon juice to kill the bacteria.
4. I'm being stalked by an annoying girl!	4. She is in my Logical Reasoning and Poetry Writing classes.
5. I creamed Amanda in a sing-off!	5. We sang all the countries of the world.
6. We put music and sports pictures on our walls.	6. They are of Beethoven and the rules of badminton.
7. Wesley says amazing things in his sleep!	7. He solves math problems.

Chapter 13

THE BRAIN BUSTER

Dear Eric,

Did you really grow half an inch? That is a pretty good amount!

I can't believe camp is already half over! Color War didn't break yet. According to our algorithm, it won't break until almost the end of camp. But I don't know about that, because it seems like that wouldn't be a surprise. But the last four years it broke at a surprising time, so maybe this year the surprise is that it will break at a not-surprising time.

Get this: Last night, Wesley solved his homework problems IN HIS SLEEP! I was up, and I heard it and wrote down the answers. Maybe tonight he'll say when Color War will break!!

Did I tell you about the brain busters? Every Monday, my counselor, David, gives us a brain buster and we have until Friday to solve it. You are only supposed to get one guess, but we figured out that you can usually get another guess if you bribe David with a Kit Kat. He really likes Kit Kats. This week's brain buster is SO SO SO hard. No one can solve it!! If you get this before Friday and you can solve it, you should call the camp and leave a message for me with the answer. Okay I'll put a copy of it here. Get ready for your brain to bust ha ha! Here it is:

You are being held prisoner in a castle. The king says he'll give you a 50-50 chance to live or die. He takes you onto a field that is covered with black and white pebbles. He says, "I am going to pick up two pebbles. In one hand I'll have a black pebble, and in one hand I'll have a white pebble. You get to pick a hand. If you choose

*the hand with the white pebble, you get to go free. But
if you choose the hand with the black pebble, you die."
You agree to the rules. He reaches down and picks up a
pebble in each hand. But you see that he secretly picked
up two black pebbles! You know that if you accuse him
of cheating, he will kill you instantly. What do you do?*

Wesley didn't solve the mystery of life in his sleep that
night, but he did say something that helped solve the weekly
brain buster.

"Okay," said Wesley during lunch. "What did I say
again?"

"First you said, 'Oh, duh,'" said Nikhil, who had heard
Wesley talk when he'd woken up to go to the bathroom. "Then
you said, 'Use the pebbles on the ground.' And then, when I
came back from the bathroom, you said, 'Opposites.'"

"It has to relate to the brain buster," said Gabe as he
chewed on a grilled cheese sandwich. "Why else would you
be talking about pebbles?"

"Unless in your dream you were in Pebbleland," joked
Nikhil.

Wesley lowered his forehead onto his tray and moaned,

"I don't remember. I could have been dreaming about Pebbleland. Once I dreamed that I was in Candyland. I was eating a really big marshmallow, and when I woke up, my pillow was gone."

Gabe and Nikhil burst out laughing. "Well," said Gabe, pushing aside his grilled cheese and the possibility of Wesley eating a pillow in his sleep, "last night you said, 'Use the pebbles on the ground,' and now we can use that to solve the weekly brain buster." He took out the copy of the brain buster that he'd been carrying in his pocket all week and put it on the table, above their trays.

"Use the pebbles on the ground . . . ," Wesley said. "How can you use the pebbles on the ground? . . ."

"What about 'opposites'?" said Gabe. "You also said 'opposites.'"

"That was after I went to the bathroom," Nikhil reminded him. "Wesley could have been in a totally different dream by then. Who knows?"

"You can't accuse him of cheating," Wesley read again.

"You could ask to see the two pebbles before you start. Just to be safe," said Nikhil. "That's what I'd do." He took a bite of his sandwich and chewed it slowly and carefully.

"You could say you get to pick the two pebbles you use," tried Gabe.

"But he already picked them." Wesley pointed to that sentence with his knife. "Now you just have to pick a hand."

Nikhil put his finger up while he chewed. He never spoke with food in his mouth, to avoid choking. "You could pick the left hand," he said after he swallowed. "And then, when it's black . . ." He trailed off.

"But that's not using the pebbles on the ground," said Gabe, picking up his cookie. "We have to try to use the pebbles on the ground, like Wesley said."

Nikhil opened his mouth to say something, but then he looked at Wesley and changed his mind.

"The ground is covered in black and white pebbles," said Wesley, onto something. "You could pick up your own white pebble . . . and then ask him to shake hands before you start?"

The counselors called for them to start cleaning up. Absorbed in thought, the boys finished their last bites and walked one behind the other to throw out their trash and deposit their trays.

"Use the pebbles on the ground," Gabe muttered. He

stopped for a second to think, and—*bonk*—Nikhil came crashing into him from behind. Gabe's grilled cheese crusts and watery ice flew into Wesley's back. Plates and cups and utensils clattered to the floor. There were a few seconds of silence as everyone in the cafeteria stopped and looked at them. But then, seeing nothing more exciting than a minor traffic accident, the noise returned.

"Sorry," said Nikhil. He rushed to the floor to start picking everything up. "I should have kept a safer following distance."

"It was my fault," said Gabe. "I stopped to think. Sorry, Wesley." He got down on his knees and began picking up utensils and used napkins.

"Is this your fork?" asked Nikhil.

"No, I already have a fork," said Gabe. "I'm missing a spoon. But we need to pick up everything anyway, so it doesn't really matter whose—"

He froze. *Use the pebbles on the ground. Opposites.* "I've got it!" Gabe shouted. "You *are* a genius, Wesley! And you're a genius, too, Nikhil, for bumping into me!"

Nikhil didn't seem pleased with his credited role in the solution. Wesley looked at Gabe with a wrinkled nose, raised eyebrows, and arched shoulders to avoid contact with his wet T-shirt.

"He picked up two black pebbles," Gabe explained. "So you pick a hand and hit it really hard to make the pebble fall out. Then you say, 'Well, we can't tell what color it was because it's *on the ground* with all of these black and white pebbles. So open your other hand, and whichever color it's *not* is what I picked!'"

Wesley nodded slowly, his face lighting up. "It'll be black still in his hand, so he'll have to admit to cheating or say you picked white."

Nikhil dropped everything from his hands onto his tray and stood up. "That's good," he said, admiring the solution, if not his present situation. "But let's talk about this when we're not in a place that could trip people."

They started giving Wesley problems to solve every night while he slept. They tried math problems and historical trivia and, of course, they asked him when Color War would break. If Gabe was sure both his bunkmates were asleep, he sometimes whispered personal questions, like "What can I do to make sure Zack likes me?" and "Even though I'm getting Zack, will I ever get a baby brother or sister, one who's more like me?"

But Nikhil and Gabe had a hard time staying awake to listen for the answers. He could say them at any time—midnight, 4:00 a.m., 6:15, or not at all—and he never remembered having said anything when he woke up. Sometimes he talked in Chinese, which was worse than not talking at all, since they couldn't understand him. One night, Gabe stayed up reading under the covers with his flashlight until 1:00 a.m., but Wesley didn't make a single sound. The next night, Wesley conducted an entire conversation with the air, but Gabe was so tired from having stayed up till one o'clock the night before that when he awoke to Wesley's voice, he just rolled over and fell back asleep.

"We need a voice recorder," said Gabe.

"But then we'd have to listen to the whole night of silence just to see if he says one thing," Nikhil pointed out. "I know. We need a sound-activated recording device. It would only kick in when there's noise."

"That would work," said Gabe. "But where do we get one of those?"

"I don't know." He brightened. "Maybe Wesley will know in his sleep!"

They presented him with the problem, but even though they ate double helpings of ice cream for extra sugar, neither Gabe nor Nikhil managed to stay awake to hear the answer.

"Anything?" Wesley asked in the morning, once he'd gotten out of his sleeping bag in 9.8 seconds.

His bunkmates shook their heads, ashamed.

Wesley's shoulders sank. "I could be curing cancer."

"Or translating the works of Shakespeare into Chinese," added Nikhil.

"Or predicting when Color War will break," reminded Gabe.

Wesley sighed. "And the world will never know."

Problem: Am I a nerd who only has nerdy adventures?

Hypothesis: No.

Proof:

THINGS I CAN TELL ZACK (I am not a nerd.)	THINGS I CAN'T TELL ZACK (I am a nerd.)
1. I'm going to sleepaway camp for six weeks!	1. It is the Summer Center for Gifted Enrichment.
2. My bunkmates are really cool, and we became friends right away!	2. They like learning digits of π.

THINGS I CAN TELL ZACK (I am not a nerd.)	THINGS I CAN'T TELL ZACK (I am a nerd.)
3. The food is bad, just like at camps in ~~books and~~ movies!	3. We fixed it with lemon juice to kill the bacteria.
4. I'm being stalked by an annoying girl!	4. She is in my Logical Reasoning and Poetry Writing classes.
5. I creamed Amanda in a sing-off!	5. We sang all the countries of the world.
6. We put music and sports pictures on our walls.	6. They are of Beethoven and the rules of badminton.
7. Wesley says amazing things in his sleep!	7. He solves math problems. 7a. and brainteasers.

Chapter 14

A NEW LOOK

Zack—

My dad said in his letter that you sent me a really cool postcard from Disneyland. I didn't get it yet, but when I do, I'm going to put it up on the wall of my bunk. Wesley put up a postcard from his cousin in China, and my friend Ashley sent me one from Boston (she went there with her family) and I put it up. Soon we'll have a whole wall of postcards!

* * *

Gabe stood with the pencil in his hand, staring at the activity list. *Just sign up for it*, he coaxed himself. He peered down the cabin to the far back wall, where the READING ROCKS poster was hanging. *This is just what you need.*

Wesley was still doing the play, and Nikhil—he moved his finger to Nikhil's name and followed the code for the activity number he'd selected—was registered for stargazing. None of the other options were calling to him, and there was no way Amanda would guess that he'd pick this one.

Wesley poked his head in the door of the cabin. "Hurry up and pick your activity, Gabe! David's going to show us how to throw a Frisbee overhand!"

Wesley disappeared as quickly as he'd come, and Gabe was left alone with his thoughts and the list. He pictured Zack's spiky, gelled hair and how cool it looked. *I can't change everything nerdy about this place, but I can change myself. I just have to do it*, he thought.

With a deep breath and a burst of confidence, he signed up for activity choice four: "Try new hairstyles."

Once he'd signed up, he didn't back down. Not when David pulled him aside at dinner and asked him to confirm his choice on the sign-up sheet, and not when he was the only boy in the "Try new hairstyles" room.

A line of mirrors hung along one wall, and a cluster of desks in the center of the room were covered in hair products and accessories. There were brushes, combs, headbands, and barrettes, plus bottles of mousse, canisters of spray, and tubs of gel. The girls talked excitedly and pointed to various items on the desks. They didn't even seem to notice Gabe, who was standing in the back, awkwardly fiddling with strings from the hood of his sweatshirt.

"Okay, listen up, please," said one of the counselors—both female—in charge. "All of these brushes and combs are new. If you use one, put your name on the handle with one of these Sharpies. No sharing brushes allowed. Also, Colleen is going to demonstrate how to use the straight irons and the curling iron. You can only use one of those after you watch the demonstration, because they get really hot and you could get burned if you don't know what you're doing. Otherwise, you're welcome to use any of the products here." She waved her arm over the array on the desks. "And we can help you French braid and reverse French braid, if you'd like."

The girls began to whisper and squeal and plan. Gabe began to wonder if he'd made a big mistake.

"Have fun!" said the counselor.

The girls swarmed the products like happy ants at a picnic, and within a few seconds most of the choices were gone. Once they'd dispersed into groups, Gabe walked up to the desks and looked over what remained. Pomade, Frizz Away, Super Ultra Hold, Max Volume—what did any of this stuff even mean? He was reading the back of a bottle of "smoothing creme" when the counselor who'd done the introduction came over and sat on the edge of the desk.

"I don't think that's your best choice," she said. "Your hair's not really long enough to need smoothing creme."

Gabe put the bottle down and stared, overwhelmed and disappointed, at the floor.

The counselor held out her hand. "I'm Francesca," she said.

"Gabe."

"Nice to meet you, Gabe. What are you looking to do here?"

Gabe gulped, his stomach flipping with worry. He knew this was a bold activity choice, but was she going to kick him out? "What do you mean?" he asked.

"I mean, what do you want your hair to look like? Do you want it bigger, parted, spiky, slicked back? If you tell me what you're looking to do, I can help you find the right product. Consider me your personal style consultant."

Relieved, Gabe looked up at Francesca for the first time and smiled. A personal style consultant—that was exactly what he needed if he wanted to look less nerdy. "My stepbrother wears his kind of spiky and messy," he said, "but on purpose."

Francesca bit her lower lip and nodded. "The tousled look. I feel you." She scanned the table and chose a tub of clear, bubble-filled gel. "Take off your glasses and have a seat." She raised her eyebrows twice in quick succession. "I'm going to work some magic."

Francesca rubbed some gel between her hands and applied it to the whole of Gabe's head first, massaging his scalp. With his glasses off, Gabe's heightened sense of touch made him tingle from the cold goopiness of the gel on his head, but he felt the way he had before reading his haiku out loud in poetry class, anxious and excited at the same time. After the initial big coating, Francesca used her fingertips to position smaller pieces of hair in different directions. Gabe could hear her pausing and considering, then feel her adjusting. When she was done, she stood him up and led him, his eyes closed and glasses in his hand, to the wall with the mirrors.

"Are you ready?" she said.

Please don't let me look like a poodle, Gabe thought.

"Take a look!"

Gabe put on his glasses and opened his eyes. He turned his head to the right and then the left. It was different, but it looked pretty good! "Do you think it looks cool?" he asked Francesca.

"I think it looks awesome," she said, "but I did it, so I'm biased. Here. Colleen!" She called the other counselor. "Come check out Gabe's hair."

Colleen put her hand over her heart and gave a long, loud gasp. "I *love* it!" she cried.

"You do?" said Gabe.

"Yes! But you know what I might love even more? A Caesar style."

"Like Julius Caesar?" said Gabe. He tried to remember what Caesar looked like.

"Oh," said Francesca, "brushed forward? But we could flip the front up. That might look slick."

Colleen sprayed Gabe's hair with water to loosen the gel and then combed it all straight toward his face. Then she knelt down and used a brush to make the front go straight up, and—after telling him to close his eyes—she sprayed a cloud of hair spray to make it hold.

Gabe thought this looked pretty good too. Even though it was named for a historical figure, it looked like a style Zack would approve of.

Francesca was at the side of the room, holding pieces of hair from two girls' heads while two other girls practiced French braiding. "I really like that," she said to Gabe.

"Let me see," said one of the girls who was having her hair braided.

Francesca and the girls shuffled over to Gabe in a clump, all attached. "Oh, yeah," said the girl. "Some boys in my school wear their hair like that."

"Now let me see," said the other girl whose hair Francesca was holding. They all shifted positions.

"My brother used to wear his hair like that," the girl said, "but now that he's in middle school he wears it kind of up in the middle instead. He says this style is so out."

"It is?" Gabe asked.

He spent the rest of activity time in the center of a group of girls, every one of them with an opinion about which hairstyle would be the coolest. His hair was side parted, center parted, slicked back, and faux hawked. They brushed, moussed, spritzed, and teased until he was sure his hair was going to fall out.

At the end, he looked at himself in the mirror. His neck was sore, his sweatshirt was wet, and his forehead was sticky.

"Well, Gabe," said Francesca, "which do you like best? Let me know and I'll even let you keep the product we used for it." She winked.

Gabe thought as he looked in the mirror. Apart from a few styles that had everyone cracking up, he thought Zack would consider a lot of them cool. "Which one did you think was the best?" he asked Francesca.

"A lot of them looked really good," she said. "But only you can decide which one is really *you*."

Gabe wrinkled his nose in the mirror. Just what he needed. Another thing to figure out.

Problem: Am I a nerd who only has nerdy adventures?

Hypothesis: No.

Proof:

THINGS I CAN TELL ZACK (I am not a nerd.)	THINGS I CAN'T TELL ZACK (I am a nerd.)
1. I'm going to sleepaway camp for six weeks!	1. It is the Summer Center for Gifted Enrichment.
2. My bunkmates are really cool, and we became friends right away!	2. They like learning digits of π.
3. The food is bad, just like at camps in ~~books and~~ movies!	3. We fixed it with lemon juice to kill the bacteria.
4. I'm being stalked by an annoying girl!	4. She is in my Logical Reasoning and Poetry Writing classes.
5. I creamed Amanda in a sing-off!	5. We sang all the countries of the world.
6. We put music and sports pictures on our walls.	6. They are of Beethoven and the rules of badminton.
7. Wesley says amazing things in his sleep!	7. He solves math problems. 7a. and brainteasers.
8. I tried some cool hairstyles that lots of girls said looked cute.	8. One is named for Julius Caesar.

Chapter 15

THE POSTCARD WALL

Dear Gabe,

Hi from Disneyland. I no Disney is
lame but I used to come here alot
when I was a kid so my mom wanted to
come 1 more time b4 we move. C the
picktur on the front that is space
montin. that ride is still good I rode
it 3 times!! Its pitch black in their
but not really scary. I like getting ur
letters from camp it sounds like the
funnest. can u beleve the wedding is

soon. after disney I have to pack all my stuf to move but I got a space moantin poster to put in our new room. talk 2 u soon!

from Zack

"Is that a postcard, Gabe?" asked Nikhil. "Add it to the postcard wall!"

"I think the postcard wall needs a theme song," said Wesley. He sang, "*Postcard waalll, poooostcard wall.*"

"Wait," said Nikhil. "We should only sing the postcard wall theme song when we add a postcard to it."

"Okay, but let me practice. *Postcard waalll, poooostcard wall. Gabe's adding a postcard to the postcard wall.*" Wesley looked at Gabe, who was staring blankly at the back of his postcard. He sang, "*Gabe's not adding a postcard to the postcard wall. He's not even listening to the postcard wall song.*"

That was true; Gabe wasn't listening. He was trying to figure out what to do with this postcard. The picture of Space Mountain was cool, and the fact that Zack said "our room" made Gabe's heart race with excitement. But Zack's spelling was so poor. And so was his grammar. And even his handwriting—it looked like he'd written it with the wrong hand. What if one of his bunkmates turned it over and saw how badly his stepbrother wrote? *It's okay,* he thought. *What's the big deal? It's not like* I *spelled "mountain" two different ways—both wrong—even though the correct spelling is printed right on the postcard, just a few inches away.*

He stood up and walked over to the postcard wall with his postcard.

Nikhil poked Wesley. "Sing it! He's putting it up."

Wesley cleared his throat. *"Postcard wall, postcard wall."*

All the postcards were taped on the top so you could flip them up and see the messages. Nikhil's eight-year-old sister had written with her postcard upside down, but Gabe remembered that her grammar was better than Zack's. Even Wesley's cousin in China had better spelling than Zack, and he was only just learning English. Gabe felt a funny, hollow feeling as he held Zack's postcard. It was similar to how he felt back in New York City with Zack, when he'd worn his skeleton pajamas—only the reverse. Here at camp, could it be that *he* was embarrassed to have a stepbrother like *Zack*?

David entered their section of the cabin and knocked

on the side of Nikhil's bed. "Dinnertime," he said. "Come on, guys, line up."

Nikhil looked at his watch. "But it's only five fifty," he said. "My watch hasn't even beeped the five-minute warning yet. And it can't be wrong; it had the same time as the computer this morning—I checked. Just to be safe."

"Your watch is right, Nikhil," said David. "But the camp director wants everyone there a little early today. She has an announcement."

Wesley dropped the book he was holding and stood up, ready to go. "Come on, guys. Announcement!"

"Maybe it has to do with Color War," said Nikhil.

"But the algorithm doesn't have it breaking until next week," said Gabe.

"The algorithm could be wrong," said Wesley.

"Guys," said David, "let's go."

With their hurry to get out and their conjecture about what the announcement could be, no one mentioned the postcard wall. Before running out to line up, Gabe folded the postcard in half—with the writing inside—and slipped it between his mattress and bed frame.

Chapter 16

PEDICULUS CAPITIS

When everyone was seated in the cafeteria, the camp director stood on a chair and spoke into a megaphone. "Everyone! Attention please."

"I think you're right, Wesley," whispered Nikhil. "She's going to break Color War!"

"I thought it's supposed to break with something crazy and fun," said Gabe, disappointed. "I'll be mad if it just starts with the director saying it at dinner."

"Quiet, guys," said their counselor.

"See?" whispered Nikhil. "You have to be quiet when Color War breaks."

The director cleared her throat into the megaphone and waited until she had complete silence. "Thank you," she said. "Unfortunately, we found a case of head lice here at Summer Center. We have treated the camper who had it, but I want all of you to be extra careful. Don't share hairbrushes or hats, and don't put your head on someone else's pillow. Shampoo every day. If you feel itchy, please see the nurse. We don't want the lice to spread. Those of you who did the hairstyles activity a few days ago should especially get checked. Any questions—" Hands shot up around the cafeteria before she could finish her sentence with "ask your counselors."

The director paused, deciding whether or not to answer questions herself. Then she called on a boy whose hand was up and shaking with urgency.

"Who has it?" he asked.

"That's not important," the director said.

"But if we know who has it," the boy explained, "we'll know who to stay away from."

The director said, "You don't need to stay away from anyone, but the point is that you should be cautious in general, because it could spread to anyone."

At Gabe's table, Nikhil nodded nervously. Gabe noticed

that he was leaning slightly away from Gabe, probably because his spiky do reminded Nikhil that he'd done the hairstyles activity.

The camp director pointed at a girl on the other side of the room. "Yes?"

"Lice are insects, right? What genus and species are they?"

The director's expression was a cross between amusement and exasperation. "I don't know," she admitted. "Thank you for your attention. If you have any other questions about how to prevent lice, please talk to your counselors or the nurse. If you have questions about lice as organisms, speak to a science teacher."

A camper seated right near the director raised her hand intently. The director looked at it, contemplating. Finally she said, "Is this a question that you could ask someone later?" The girl shook her head, and the director said, "Okay, last question, then. Go ahead."

"I don't know the genus and species, but I do know the phylum and class," the girl said. "Anthropoda Insecta."

"Thank you," said the director. "Let's all be vigilant so the lice won't be a problem. Have a great day."

Gabe remembered how many girls had touched his head

at the hairstyles activity. All of a sudden, his scalp felt itchy. He didn't seem to be the only one.

"I think I've got it," Nikhil said. He ran his hands through his tall yard of hair as though searching for something he'd buried there earlier. "I should probably go see the nurse."

"Do lice fly?" Wesley wondered aloud.

"I don't think so," said Gabe, running his pointer fingers over his scalp. "I know they lay eggs, though."

"But they're insects," said Wesley. He asked their counselor, "Do lice have wings?"

Gabe asked, "Is 'lice' the same singular and plural?"

Nikhil ran a fork through his hair and examined the prongs. "I should probably just shave my head," he said. "Just to be safe."

The nighttime activity choices changed every day, but they usually fell into standard categories: arts, crafts, sports, academic challenges. But every now and then there'd be a special activity, brought on by extraordinary circumstances and only available that one time. The night Gabe had tried different hairstyles, for instance, was particularly clear, so Nikhil had done stargazing. And the day a famous chef came to speak to the Food Science class, he stuck around for activities and taught campers how to make cinnamon rolls.

On the sign-up sheet the day after the director's announcement, there was an ad for another special, one-time activity.

DUE TO POPULAR DEMAND, THE NURSE AND SCIENCE TEACHERS PROUDLY PRESENT . . .

LICE 101

- Learn all about *Pediculus humanus capitis* before we expel it from camp!

- Get your questions answered!

- Prevention tips and tricks, real-lice horror stories, anatomy and breeding—we've got it all!

ONE NIGHT ONLY! SPACE IS LIMITED! SIGN UP NOW!

The counselors didn't know how many people would sign up, but they reserved one of the larger science rooms so that they could fit up to thirty campers. Once the sign-up sheets were collected, they had to trade rooms with the theater group so they could hold Lice 101 in the amphitheater, the only space that could comfortably accommodate eighty- three people.

Gabe and Nikhil both went, even though the nurse had given them each a clean bill of health the night before (and that morning again for Nikhil; he'd gotten checked twice). Amanda came in with Jenny Chin, and they sat right in front of Gabe and Nikhil on the risers, so that Amanda's long, puffy hair hung millimeters from Gabe's shins.

One of the science teachers stood in the center of the stage and expressed her excitement at having so many people interested in head lice. She began with some facts: "*Pediculus humanus capitis*, commonly referred to as head lice, are wingless insects that feed on human blood. They are about the size of sesame seeds. They have six legs that have claws that grip human hair."

Gabe looked at the back of Amanda's head. It was a thick, frizzy blob, a *Pediculus humanus capitis* amusement park.

The science teacher began writing and drawing on a rolling whiteboard that had been brought in for the occasion. She said, "The eggs that lice lay are called nits. Nits are oval in shape, and they're sort of yellowish white. When a female louse—'louse' is the singular for 'lice'—lays her eggs, the eggs glue themselves to the hair shaft."

Gabe pulled his legs up onto the seat, away from Amanda's hair.

The teacher wrote THE LIFE CYCLE OF LICE on the board and began drawing a diagram. A few campers started to take notes. Gabe watched with interest, being careful to keep his toes away from Amanda's hair. He'd always lined up for the yearly lice check at school, and the one or two times someone in his class had it, he'd stuffed the note about it in his take-home folder with all the other handouts for his mom. He'd never really thought about lice as living organisms until today.

As he listened to the science teacher answer questions from around the room, he felt a tingly feeling come over him that he could only attribute to a love of Summer Center and everything they did there. For the sake of his logic proof, he knew he should bury that feeling and cover it up tightly.

Gabe ran his hands over the stiff peaks he'd spent ten minutes forming on his head. *Is it really fair that I have to stop liking Summer Center to please someone who thinks "picture" is spelled "picktur"?*

"No," said the teacher, "lice can't survive more than twenty-four hours without a human host. They need human blood to live."

"That's gross but also cool," Nikhil whispered to Gabe. "They're like little vampires. Not that vampires are real."

Gabe put his fingers on his top lip to make fangs, and Nikhil covered his head with his arms. A printout with a blown-up picture of a real louse reached Amanda in front of them, and Gabe and Nikhil looked between the girls' shoulders to get a peek. "Look at its claws," said Gabe.

Amanda spun around and smiled. "I know you like doing things with me, but you should wait for your turn."

Gabe bared his teeth and made his thumb and pointer finger into lice pinchers. Amanda stuck out her tongue and turned back around.

Now the nurse took the stage to begin talking about preventing the spread of lice. "Girls with long hair should be especially careful. It's probably a good idea to wear your hair in braids and wear a hat or a bandanna over it."

Gabe sat back and thought about how he could turn the lice problem into an epic poem. He could make it a whole story about killer lice vampires that are sucking the blood of unknown victims at camp. It would be really exciting, with plot twists and fight scenes and a team of bandanna-clad combs that blast the nits into oblivion. *What rhymes with lice?* he thought. *Mice, rice, nice, suffice. . . .* He kind of hoped that the lice stuck around camp a little longer. Imagine a whole lice epidemic! That'd even be something he could write to Zack about—it was like something straight out of the *Grossology* book—as long as he didn't catch it himself. Fighting to obliterate lice was cool. Catching lice was not.

"Thanks for coming to Lice 101!" said the nurse. "You are all smart kids. If you're smart about preventing lice, this camp will be a lice-free zone the rest of the summer. You can *head* back to your bunks—ha-ha!"

Problem: Am I a nerd who only has nerdy adventures?

Hypothesis: No.

Proof:

THINGS I CAN TELL ZACK (I am not a nerd.)	THINGS I CAN'T TELL ZACK (I am a nerd.)
1. I'm going to sleepaway camp for six weeks!	1. It is the Summer Center for Gifted Enrichment.
2. My bunkmates are really cool, and we became friends right away!	2. They like learning digits of π.
3. The food is bad, just like at camps in ~~books and~~ movies!	3. We fixed it with lemon juice to kill the bacteria.

130

THINGS I CAN TELL ZACK (I am not a nerd.)	THINGS I CAN'T TELL ZACK (I am a nerd.)
4. I'm being stalked by an annoying girl!	4. She is in my Logical Reasoning and Poetry Writing classes.
5. I creamed Amanda in a sing-off!	5. We sang all the countries of the world.
6. We put music and sports pictures on our walls.	6. They are of Beethoven and the rules of badminton.
7. Wesley says amazing things in his sleep!	7. He solves math problems. 7a. and brainteasers.
8. I tried some cool hairstyles that lots of girls said looked cute.	8. One is named for Julius Caesar.
9. Vampire lice are sucking the blood out of people's heads!	9. We learned all about the *Pediculus humanus capitis* and their life cycle.

Chapter 17

C² AND THE DOUBLE L

Dear Ashley,

You know how in my last letter I told you about the lice war? Even though in the poem I wrote, Super Combman and the Shampolice destroyed the lice, in real life the war is still raging. Don't worry, I don't have it and no one in my bunk does. But a lot of girls have it, and even a boy in another bunk got it! Yesterday, we got another talk about how to prevent it. All the girls have to wear bandannas, and all the boys have to wear hats all the time now. It seems like the counselors and the nurse are really confused.

No one can figure out why it's still around, not even Wesley in his sleep. These lice are tough! We play Lice vs. Hair during recess. It's kind of like tag, but the person who's It is lice and everyone else is Hair. It's fun.

It was probably the sign that doomed Gabe's bunk. The very day their counselor taped a sign to the cabin door that said BUNK 2B IS A LICE-FREE ZONE, Victor Kim started scratching his head. No one noticed it at first because Victor was a thoughtful kid who scratched his head whenever he asked a question. But he scratched and then tossed Robby the hat he'd forgotten on his way out of the bunk. And then Robby dried his hair after swimming in the lake and dropped his towel on top of Justin's. And then Justin told Nikhil he thought he had a mosquito bite on his head, and Nikhil took a big step away from him and sent him to the nurse.

Their counselor took down the sign.

"The lice should be totally gone by now," Nikhil lamented, "not invading our bunk!"

Wesley reached to scratch his head but thought better of it. "It is weird. It seems like everyone is doing what they're supposed to, but the lice keep spreading."

"It's a mystery," Gabe agreed. Even he, who'd wished for an epidemic, thought this lice situation was getting old. It was annoying to have to think about his hair all the time and to listen to Nikhil freak out over every regular itch. He'd even stopped gelling his hair in the mornings, afraid to touch his head too much. The only good thing about lice was that a whole group of girls in Amanda's bunk had it at some point, so it gave him a valid excuse to keep away from her. But somewhere deep in his brain he admitted that he'd rather combat Amanda Wisznewski than head lice. At least she kept things interesting.

"I wonder if they won't break Color War until the lice are gone," said Wesley. "The algorithm has it starting at the end of the week, but all the counselors are so busy shampooing people."

Gabe had a scary thought. "What if there's lice until the end of the summer and they have to *cancel* Color War?"

"We have to stop it from spreading," said Nikhil. "Maybe if Wesley takes a nap right now, he'll tell us how."

But Wesley was hesitant to put his head on his pillow. Everything in the cabin looked dangerous. Pillows and sleeping bags, clothing, towels—even books and calculators could be infested.

Gabe said, "I kind of wish I'd just catch it already so I could stop living in fear. If *everyone* had lice, we could just have Color War, because there'd be no danger of anyone new catching it."

Nikhil glared at him to take it back.

Wesley shook his lice-free head. "Yeah, but it's not like chicken pox, where you get it once and then can't ever get it again. Like Jenny Chin. She got it in the beginning, and then, after the nurse finally said she was clean, she got it again."

"That is fishy . . . ," Gabe said. He had an idea. "Maybe Combman and the Shampolice aren't superheroes—they're detectives in the Case of the Returning Lice. And the first suspect is Jenny Chin."

Wesley raised his hand. "Can I be Combman?" he asked.

"No," said Nikhil, "Gabe gets to be Combman because he invented him. We're just his sidekicks."

"The Shampolice," said Gabe.

"Can I be chief of the Shampolice?" asked Wesley. Nikhil shrugged, and Wesley said, "Yes! Chief of the Shampolice reporting for duty. What do we do, Combman?"

"Investigate," said Gabe. "We need to question the suspect."

* * *

The questioning took place the next day during free time. They all met at a picnic table in the woods, and anyone who came by chasing a Frisbee or looking for a quiet place to read apologized and ran off, since it was clear that the meeting was official. The suspect wore a bathing suit beneath her tank top and shorts. At Amanda's suggestion, Jenny refused to talk without legal counsel present, so she was joined by Amanda, who looked the part in a big T-shirt with the name of her father's law firm on the pocket. Both girls had their hair in two French braids beneath bandannas, Jenny's red and Amanda's tie-dyed.

On the other side of the table, the detectives all wore shorts and T-shirts. Combman sat in the middle, wearing a New York Mets hat. The Shampolice officers sat on either side of him. The chief was wearing a khaki fisherman's hat that said FAN FAMILY REUNION on the front. He had a notebook and pencil to take notes. The other officer was wearing a shower cap with masking tape around the elastic. Just to be safe.

"I call this meeting to order," said Wesley. He tapped his pencil eraser against his notebook like a gavel.

"This isn't court," said Jenny.

"No, but it's just as important that you tell the truth," said Wesley.

Jenny and Amanda looked at each other as if to say, *Boys*.

Amanda folded her hands on the table. "You had some questions for my client?"

Gabe nodded. "We are investigating the Mystery of the Returning Lice, and your client is our first suspect."

"Suspect!" said Jenny. "Try victim."

"Jenny," warned Amanda. She looked at Gabe. "My client objects to the term 'suspect.' She is a blameless victim of lice."

"Twice?" said Wesley with his eyebrows raised.

Jenny crossed her arms. "You think I *wanted* to catch lice twice?"

"I'm sure we can clear your name," said Nikhil. "We're investigating everyone right now," he explained. "Just to be safe."

Gabe looked to either side of him, impressed with the good-cop-bad-cop routine his roommates had worked out without even planning it. That meant he, Combman, could just play it straight and ask the questions. "Do you have any idea how you caught lice the first time?" he asked Jenny.

She shrugged. "All these girls in my bunk got it. It could have been from anything."

"What about the second time?" Gabe asked.

Jenny glanced at Amanda and then looked down at the table and shrugged again.

She's hiding something! Gabe thought. "After you got it the first time and the nurse gave you the shampoo treatments, how long was it before you got it again?"

Jenny did some math in her head. "Three days."

"Did a lot of other people in your bunk still have it in those three days, so you could catch it?"

"Not really," Jenny admitted. "Everyone got shampooed."

Wesley stood up and leaned over the table. "So, where'd you get it from the second time, then, huh? Tell us or we'll throw you in the slammer!"

Amanda stood up. "Objection! Don't try to intimidate my client."

"Take it easy, Wesley," said Gabe.

"If you can't keep your boys in line, this is over," said Amanda.

"I'm sorry," said Nikhil. "We're just trying to get to the bottom of this."

Wesley sat down, but his suspicious eyes didn't leave Jenny for a second. She stuck out her tongue at him.

Gabe summoned all he knew about police interrogations from TV and books and tried again. "Even though it may seem like it from my partner here"—he motioned to his right—"no one is accusing you of anything. We're just wondering if you can give us any clues about why the lice won't go away. Think hard, Jenny. Did you do anything that might have caused you to get it again in those three days?"

Jenny looked at Gabe and Wesley. She pulled her lips back and forth in consideration. Then she looked at Nikhil with his masking-taped shower cap and started giggling. "Can I have a minute to consult with my lawyer?" she asked.

"Okay," said Gabe. The boys got up and walked a few feet away. They quizzed one another on various digits of Pi until the girls called them back to the table.

Amanda said, "My client would like to make a deal. In exchange for her information, she'd like three books, two Twizzlers, and a Snickers bar."

Gabe let out a low whistle. Wesley threw his arms up. "*Three* books! How do we even know if her information is good?"

"It's good," said Jenny.

Nikhil whispered, "Let's do it. I don't *think* they'd cancel Color War because of the lice, but we have to try to get rid of them, just in case. Besides, this masking tape hurts."

Wesley whispered, "But I'm down to my second-to-last Snickers."

"Two books," said Gabe firmly. "Two Twizzlers. No Snickers."

The girls looked at each other.

"Deal," said Amanda.

"Let's go," said Jenny.

The boys looked at one another.

"Where are we going?" asked Nikhil.

"The place I went in the three days before I caught lice again. Come on."

She led them through the woods, across the field, past the bunks, and to the front of the science building.

"You're not supposed to be in classrooms during free time," said Nikhil.

Jenny ignored him. She opened the door and walked inside. The others hurried to catch up with her. Up the stairs, down the hall, and around the corner, she stopped at a door between rooms 222 and 224. Unlike the classroom doors, which had large windows on top, this door was solid wood. Jenny put her finger to her lips. The five of them stood silently. Gabe closed his eyes, and he could make out muffled noises from behind the door. *Something top secret is going on in there,* he thought.

"You guys move over there," Jenny whispered. She straightened her bandanna. Then she raised her fist and knocked in a beat: *Tap.* Pause. *Tap-tap.* Pause. *Tap.*

A secret-code knock, Gabe thought. *This I definitely have to tell Zack.*

There was some shuffling behind the door, and the boys waited, Gabe and Wesley with eager anticipation, and Nikhil with a combination of curiosity and fear. Finally, the door opened just enough to let a single eye peer through the crack and see Jenny. Then the door opened halfway and a hand waved Jenny in. She beckoned the rest of the group to follow her and said, "Come on, guys."

They walked inside what seemed to be a deep janitor's closet. Piled on the floor were buckets and cleaning supplies. A few janitor uniforms were hanging from hooks along the left wall. But it was what was along the right wall that made Gabe's eyes widen behind his glasses. There was a long table, but all the cleaning products were pushed together far from the door. In their place were two microscopes, an array of petri dishes, and a pyramid of glass jars labeled with black marker.

Gabe was so absorbed with the makeshift lab that he didn't even notice the other person who was in there until he spoke.

"Uh, Jen," the guy said. "What are you doing?"

Gabe looked at this guy and wondered if his thick glasses were deceiving him. He was one of the older kids, but he wasn't just any older kid. He was Calvin Chin, C^2.

Everyone knew C^2. He was the smartest of the smartest of the smart kids at Smart Camp. He had skipped third grade and then sixth. So now, at thirteen, he had already completed one year of high school and was smart enough to be starting college. But he had lots of friends in his current grade, and his parents wanted him to have a normal teenage life, so he wasn't going to skip any more. That made him the best combination: a thirteen-year-old who was college smart and high school cool. He was a legend! And talk about cool: His nickname represented the hypotenuse of a right triangle *and* the speed of light. *Zack would think that's nerdy*, Gabe thought, *but C² wouldn't even care.*

C² was wearing a white lab apron and, like Nikhil, a shower cap. But unlike Nikhil, he somehow managed to make the shower cap look so good that Gabe wished he had one himself.

"Guys," said Jenny, "this is my brother Calvin."

Brother! Gabe thought. *Of course!* Why hadn't he put it together that Jenny Chin and Calvin Chin were brother and sister? If he had known Jenny was related to C², he would have tried to hang out with her more, and even with Amanda.

C² said, "Hey," and lifted his chin at the group to acknowledge them. Then he looked back at his sister. "I told you not to bring anyone here."

"Yeah," she said, "but they were investigating the lice thing, and we made a deal. Besides, I'm tired of lice. I told you, if you don't shut it down today, I'm going to tell my counselor."

C² sighed and shook his head.

"What is all this stuff?" asked Wesley.

"It's the Double L," C² said proudly. "The Lice Lab. Some friends and I got it going. We got specimens from this girl's hair, and then we set it up to do some experiments."

"What sorts of experiments?" asked Gabe.

"Just looking at them on slides, breeding them in jars, seeing how they act if you feed them different things. That sort of stuff."

"Cool," said Gabe.

"Do the teachers know?" asked Nikhil. "How'd you get the microscopes and stuff?"

"We took the petri dishes and jars from a few science rooms, and we've been bringing the microscopes back and forth from one of the labs."

"You mean, you stole them?" asked Nikhil.

C^2 shrugged. "It's in the name of science. But it's probably a good idea to shut it down and disinfect all the equipment now, anyway. Now that everybody knows and tons of people are coming here to look, *Jenny*."

"Whatever," said Jenny. "You're the one *breeding* lice and feeding them to keep them alive while the rest of the camp is trying to kill them and wondering why they keep coming back."

Free time was almost over, but before they went to line up for dinner, C^2 gave them a tour of the lab and let them look at the lice through the microscope. The lice were intricate little bugs with six claws, like tiny, hairy crustaceans. *Between solving the mystery, hanging out with C², and seeing a real louse under a microscope*, Gabe thought, *this was officially the best free time ever.*

C² kept his word—he shut down the lice lab the next day during free time. But Nikhil still made sure Jenny told her counselor, who then sent the nurse to make sure everything was sterilized. C² and his friends got in some sort of trouble for operating it illegally, but part of the punishment was to go present to the science classes about what they found. By the end of activity time the next night, everyone at camp knew about the lice culprits.

"Well," Gabe said that night in their bunk, "Combman and the Shampolice helped crack the case."

"But Jenny totally tricked us," said Wesley. "She got those books and Twizzlers even though we would have found out."

"That was pretty smart," Nikhil granted.

"Figures," said Gabe. "Her brother is C²!"

"And *we* hung out with him during free time," bragged Wesley.

"And did you see what he was wearing?" Nikhil said with a grin. He ran his fingers along his head, where he still had a red mark from the masking tape. "That guy's got style!"

145

Problem: Am I a nerd who only has nerdy adventures?

Hypothesis: No.

Proof:

THINGS I CAN TELL ZACK (I am not a nerd.)	THINGS I CAN'T TELL ZACK (I am a nerd.)
1. I'm going to sleepaway camp for six weeks!	1. It is the Summer Center for Gifted Enrichment.
2. My bunkmates are really cool, and we became friends right away!	2. They like learning digits of π.
3. The food is bad, just like at camps in ~~books and~~ movies!	3. We fixed it with lemon juice to kill the bacteria.
4. I'm being stalked by an annoying girl!	4. She is in my Logical Reasoning and Poetry Writing classes.
5. I creamed Amanda in a sing-off!	5. We sang all the countries of the world.
6. We put music and sports pictures on our walls.	6. They are of Beethoven and the rules of badminton.
7. Wesley says amazing things in his sleep!	7. He solves math problems. 7a. and brainteasers.
8. I tried some cool hairstyles that lots of girls said looked cute.	8. One is named for Julius Caesar.

THINGS I CAN TELL ZACK (I am not a nerd.)	THINGS I CAN'T TELL ZACK (I am a nerd.)
9. Vampire lice are sucking the blood out of people's heads!	9. We learned all about the *Pediculus humanus capitis* and their life cycle.
10. I discovered a top secret operation!	10. It was an operation to study the science of lice.
11. I hung out with the coolest guy at camp!	11. His nickname is C^2, and he is so smart, he skipped two grades.

Chapter 18

ALIEN INVASION

Dear Eric,

It is two days past when our algorithm predicted that
Color War would break. We only have one week left
of camp now. I wish it would break the very last day
and then they would extend camp so we could have it.
I wish that because I am having so much fun and don't
want to leave. I think thinking about going home soon is
making me have weird dreams lately. But I know from
Logical Reasoning that it's not logical for Color War
to happen after camp is supposed to end.

Here is something funny about Logical Reasoning though. One property that you use in a logic proof is called Modus Tollens. Modus Tollens is not a person, it's a mathematical theorem. But here is the funny thing: Today, during our break, a girl in my class wrote "Modus Tollens wuz here" on the white board. HA HA HA HA! It was so funny that then this other kid and I tried to put her name and Modus Tollens in a heart on a tree, but we didn't have anything sharp enough to carve it.

In case you're wondering, here's an example of how Modus Tollens really works:

Given:
If our algorithm is right, then Color War would
        break on Friday.
Color War did not break on Friday.

Therefore, because of Modus Tollens:
Our algorithm was not right. ⌣̈

Gabe fell asleep quickly, but he kept waking up between weird dreams. In one, he and Amanda were on the *Titanic*, and his old babysitter was trying to teach them how to dance the fox-trot. In another, he was in his cabin, but it was really the cereal aisle of the supermarket, and he had been assigned to do a book report about the Rice Krispies box, but he was completely unprepared. In a third, his mom, who looked like his swimming coach, was trying to convince him that they should get a pet ferret.

So, when a white light swept over the bunk windows and people began waking up, it took Gabe a few minutes to realize that it wasn't just another strange dream. The boys in other parts of the cabin were whispering, but Gabe could hear them.

"What is it?"

"I don't know. Go wake up David."

"You wake him up."

"No, you do it."

Gabe rubbed his eyes and put on his glasses. The Indiglo on his watch made him squint. It was 4:02 a.m. He groaned, put his glasses back beside his bed, and closed his eyes. But the light swept across the bunk window again, illuminating the darkness behind his eyes, and he opened them again.

"There it is again," said one of the boys from the area next to Gabe's.

"Shh, do you hear that?" said another.

"Hear what?"

"Shh!"

Everyone who was awake or, like Gabe, semi-awake, listened. There was a faint hum, like someone had started the air-conditioning in another room.

Above Gabe, Wesley stirred. "Police!" he said as he turned over.

A boy gasped. "Police!" he repeated. "The lights!"

"It could be a helicopter," someone else said. "Maybe someone escaped from jail and they're looking for him."

"What *time* is it?" asked someone groggily.

"Four in the morning," Gabe answered.

"It's the police," someone said with certainty. "Ninety-four percent of jailbreaks take place between three and five in the morning."

Gabe shuddered. "Nikhil," he whispered. "Nikhil!"

"Mmm," said Nikhil.

"Wake up." Gabe sat up and nudged his head into Wesley's mattress. "Wesley, wake up."

"What is it?" mumbled Nikhil.

The light swept by the windows again, brighter this time,

and for longer. As it passed, the faint hum escalated into a loud whir, like someone had now turned up the air conditioner to full blast. Nikhil opened his eyes wide. "What is it?" he asked again, alert now.

"It's the police," answered someone who hadn't spoken before. "They're looking for an escaped convict."

"Why would a convict need to know the volume of a sphere?" said Wesley, who wasn't completely awake yet.

Nikhil was sitting straight up and gripping the edge of the bed tightly with both hands. "It's probably just people with flashlights," he said. "But I'm going to wake up David. Just to be safe."

The light came by, illuminating the room enough so that Nikhil didn't need a flashlight as he walked down the length of the bunk to the front, where the counselor's bed was. Despite the thundering whir, which was now punctuated with beeps, Nikhil's gasp was audible through the whole cabin. "David's not in his bed!" he shouted.

Now everyone began talking at once.

"Where is he?"

"They got him!"

"No, he's hiding."

"Our counselor's a convict!"

"Someone go outside and see what's going on," said Gabe.

Everyone became silent, too scared to go.

Wesley freed himself from his sleeping bag and climbed down from his bed. "We'll do it," he said.

"We?" asked Gabe.

"Yeah, us," said Wesley. "Me, you, and Nikhil. We're fearless. Come on."

Gabe swallowed hard. Then he stood up and slipped his feet into his sandals. The two of them walked through the cabin, past the two sections of bunks, from which boys looked at them with fear, admiration, and relief that someone else had volunteered. They met Nikhil at the front of the cabin and stood in silence, each wordlessly urging the others to open the door.

"On three," said Gabe. "One . . ."

"Two . . . ," said Nikhil.

"Three!" said Wesley.

They pulled open the door, and the whole cabin was drenched in light. Gabe shaded his eyes with his hand and squinted into the brightness. There were groups of campers in front of every cabin, all wearing their pajamas and in some combination of grogginess, confusion, and panic. The whirring and beeping became more intense, and the bright light suddenly went dead, revealing in the sky a flat, circular object, like an enormous hockey puck with three spotlights sticking out the bottom.

"Whoa," Nikhil said.

"Whoa squared," said Gabe. "It's a UFO."

A cold breeze blew through the camp, and Gabe felt the hairs on his arms stand up. It was cold in the middle of the night, and he hadn't thought to put on his sweatshirt.

The rest of the boys from their cabin came trickling out, as did campers from all the other cabins. Everyone stared up at the flashing lights. Even though the counselors weren't around to tell campers what to do, no one moved from their posts in front of their cabins, which left all of Shady Field clear for a UFO landing. The campers became silent as the disk descended, slowly, easily, until it gracefully touched down in the center of the field. The field lights came on, and a door opened on one side of the ship. Out came a creature wearing a reflective silver suit.

"Aliens," whispered Wesley.

But as the creature hoisted itself up to stand on the top of the spaceship, someone else had a different explanation.

"That's my Rocket Science teacher!" a girl shouted.

Gabe wiped his glasses on his shirt and put them back on. He had no idea what was going on, but he didn't want to miss one detail.

The speakers around the field crackled with feedback, and all the kids covered their ears. The feedback was then replaced by noise, as though someone was speaking but in beeps: *Beep! Beep beep-beep beep.* "Greetings, campers of SCGE," a robotic voice translated.

A cheer broke out on the side of the field where the older kids' bunks were. Gabe looked around at his bunkmates, and he was relieved to see they were all as confused but enthralled as he was.

Beep-beep-beep. BEEP! Beepbeepbeep. "We come from a faraway solar system. Your camp is known throughout our galaxy for having intelligent hu-man entities."

This time, more people cheered, including Wesley and some of the other boys from Gabe's bunk.

Beeeeeeeeeeeep. "We cannot have a group of hu-mans who are smarter than us alien beings." *Beep beep.* "We tried to destroy you with head lice, but it didn't work."

Everyone laughed and cheered, including the few people who were still wearing bandannas, even to sleep.

Beep-beep. Beep. "So we have captured your leaders—you call them counselors."

Nikhil covered his mouth with his hand.

B-beep-beep-BEEP-beep beep. "We have altered their brain waves. Now they are leaders of different nations. Each nation is a color."

Gabe smiled and felt his heart beat faster. He was starting to catch on.

Beep beeeep-beep beep beep beep. Beep. Beep beep b-beep. "The nations will war against one another. Once you intelligent hu-man entities have destroyed one another, we alien beings can take over the universe."

The camp erupted into cheers. A chant broke out from the upper cabins and spread until everyone was chanting together: "Co-lor War! Co-lor War!"

Gabe shouted along with the crowd. This was the craziest, most utterly awesome thing he had ever seen. This totally topped all the stories he'd heard about how Color War had broken in past years. What could possibly be better than a fully functioning flying saucer operated by the Rocket Science teacher?

BEEP BEEP BEEP! came the alien language over the speakers. "Here are your counselors."

"Katie White. Bunk 2A. Blue Nation."

Amanda's counselor came running out of the spaceship while all her campers shrieked and applauded. She was wearing a reflective suit that was neon blue. In one hand she waved a large neon blue flag, and in the other she carried a blue bag. When she reached her girls, she reached into the bag and started throwing blue T-shirts to them.

Next up was Francesca, the counselor who'd helped Gabe with his hair. She was dressed head to toe in yellow, and her campers shrieked as she distributed yellow T-shirts and waved the Yellow Nation flag.

Beep-BEEP-beep. Beep. "David Kilpatrick. Bunk 2B. Green Nation."

Gabe threw his arms in the air and jumped up and down along with the rest of his bunk as David burst out of the spaceship and ran toward them, decked out in green. When Gabe got his neon green shirt, he put it on right then, on top of his pajamas. It had a picture of a UFO beaming lights on the words SCGE COLOR WAR 2011.

The process repeated with the remaining counselors until the entire camp was divided into four big teams: Green, Yellow, Blue, and Red. The spaceship drove off along the grass toward the lake, while the now-warring nations shouted their colors as loudly as they could, trying to drown one another out. Once the spaceship was out of sight, a thunderous boom silenced the chants. It was coming from the lake, where green, yellow, blue, and red fireworks shot up into the dark sky.

When the fireworks ended, the counselors, shiny suits and all, led the riled-up campers back to their cabins, where they were somehow supposed to go back to sleep.

"What time is it?" asked Wesley.

Gabe checked his watch. "Four forty-five."

"In the *morning*?" said Wesley, as though it could possibly be four forty-five in the afternoon.

"That was the coolest Color War break ever," said Nikhil. "So much better than the director announcing it at dinner."

"So much better," Gabe agreed. "At first I was really scared."

"With the lights and the noise!" said Nikhil.

"Yeah, at four in the morning! I was like, what is going on?"

"I wasn't scared," said Wesley.

Gabe looked at Nikhil as if to say, *Yeah, right.* "Even when we thought it was the police looking for someone who broke out of jail?"

"I didn't believe it," said Wesley.

"But there is no escaped convict, right?" said Nikhil.

Wesley and Gabe laughed and shook their heads.

"I know. I was just making sure."

Back in the bunk, Wesley and Gabe climbed into their beds with their green T-shirts on, but Nikhil took his off and folded it neatly. Just to be safe.

"I can't believe we have to wake up in two hours and forty minutes," Gabe moaned.

"Maybe they'll let us sleep later," said Nikhil.

"Maybe the first Color War challenge is to see who can sleep the latest," said Wesley.

"I love Color War," said Gabe. Even though he had only experienced the very beginnings of it, it was true. People would be talking about what happened tonight all day tomorrow—well, later today. It was a legitimately awesome entry for the left column of his logic proof. He could tell Zack about all of it—the flying saucer and the robot voice and the fireworks and the middle of the night, but maybe not the Rocket Science teacher part—without worrying that it made him look like a nerd. And even if there was something geeky about it, nothing Zack could say could take away how much fun this night was.

"I'm so *pumped*," said Wesley. "There's no way I can go back to sleep."

"Me squared," said Nikhil.

"Me cubed," said Gabe.

But Gabe yawned. And then Wesley yawned. And then Gabe yawned again.

And within five minutes, the citizens of the Green Nation were all sound asleep.

Problem: Am I a nerd who only has nerdy adventures?

Hypothesis: No.

Proof:

THINGS I CAN TELL ZACK (I am not a nerd.)	THINGS I CAN'T TELL ZACK (I am a nerd.)
1. I'm going to sleepaway camp for six weeks!	1. It is the Summer Center for Gifted Enrichment.
2. My bunkmates are really cool, and we became friends right away!	2. They like learning digits of π.
3. The food is bad, just like at camps in ~~books and~~ movies!	3. We fixed it with lemon juice to kill the bacteria.
4. I'm being stalked by an annoying girl!	4. She is in my Logical Reasoning and Poetry Writing classes.

THINGS I CAN TELL ZACK (I am not a nerd.)	THINGS I CAN'T TELL ZACK (I am a nerd.)
5. I creamed Amanda in a sing-off!	5. We sang all the countries of the world.
6. We put music and sports pictures on our walls.	6. They are of Beethoven and the rules of badminton.
7. Wesley says amazing things in his sleep!	7. He solves math problems. 7a. and brainteasers.
8. I tried some cool hairstyles that lots of girls said looked cute.	8. One is named for Julius Caesar.
9. Vampire lice are sucking the blood out of people's heads!	9. We learned all about the *Pediculus humanus capitis* and their life cycle.
10. I discovered a top secret operation!	10. It was an operation to study the science of lice.
11. I hung out with the coolest guy at camp!	11. His nickname is C^2, and he is so smart, he skipped two grades.
12. Color War broke with aliens landing in the middle of the night!	12. Our algorithm was off by a few days.

Chapter 19

CRASH LANDING

Dear Gabe,

Did color war brake yet? I bet it brakes like a suprise. what kind of games do u play in color war is it just like sports and stuf. I hope u win and beat that girl Amanda! also ur dad told me that ur mom has a suprise 4 u when she picks u up at camp. I no what it is but I won't tell u. this is probbuly my last letter 2 u cuz u r going home soon. R u ready for the wedding?

Most mornings, the siren would sound at seven thirty and the campground itself would be just waking up. The air would be cool and moist, the grass would be damp, and the sun would duck in and out of clouds, rubbing its eyes and shaking off sleep, just like the groggy campers. But the morning after Color War broke, the siren didn't go off until ten. The sun was high and bright, the dew had dissipated, and the air was hot. The day was in full force, and that's how Gabe felt as he folded up Zack's letter, pulled on some shorts, and smoothed out his green T-shirt: refreshed and ready to tackle anything.

"If it was a regular day," he said with his mouth full of toothpaste, "we'd be almost halfway done with our morning class already!"

"It'd be almost time for lunch," said Wesley. He put down his toothbrush and looked at his bunkmates in the mirror. "Weird."

"I hope breakfast is breakfast food, though," said Nikhil. "It's the most important meal of the day."

Breakfast wasn't just breakfast food; it was breakfast food divided by nation. There were four trays of everything: scrambled eggs dyed blue, green, and red, and regular yellow. Tater Tots dyed blue, green, red, and regular yellow. Oatmeal dyed blue, green, red, and yellow. Even the fruit was divided: strawberries for red, grapes for green, bananas for yellow, and blueberries for blue. The only things that weren't divided were the orange juice and hot chocolate, and that was okay because orange and brown were neutral.

After filling up on green food and neutral drinks, the boys went with the rest of their division out to Shady Field, just like they would on school days. Only today, they weren't lining up by class and going into the classrooms; they were lining up by team and finding out which battle they would face first. A large scoreboard listed all the upcoming battles and how many points each was worth.

BATTLE	TOTAL POINTS
Field day	200
Scavenger hunt	400
Water sports	200
Obstacle course	200
Jeopardy!	400
Sing-off	400
Team spirit	200
Sportsmanship	200

After a spontaneous chanting battle between the different teams, the older kids from each nation headed to the lake for

164

water sports, while Gabe and the other younger kids stayed on the field for field day.

Amanda snaked through the crowd until she found Gabe. She put her arm around his shoulders. "I bet you wish I was on Green with you," she said. "But you're going down."

"We're enemies," Gabe said, realizing what was perhaps the best part of the next two days. "I can't talk to you."

Green Nation had a strong showing for field day. A boy from Gabe's bunk blasted to victory in the fifty-yard dash, earning Green 30 points. Then Gabe and Wesley were the stars of the three-legged race: They blazed past a team of boys from Yellow at the very end to come in second place, just behind a pair of girls from Red, which gave them another 10. Then the counselors brought out large soil-sample bags from the Earth Science class to use for a potato-sack race. Wesley, who apparently had a hidden talent for jumping far and fast, came in first, bringing the team's total to 70.

The water-balloon toss seemed like another sure victory for Green. Nikhil handled everything with caution just to be safe, so he was a pro at throwing and catching breakable things. Paired with thoughtful Victor Kim, who cupped the water balloon with such tenderness, it could have been a living creature, they were a water-balloon-toss dream team. After a few rounds of poor throws and clumsy catches, the competition was whittled down to two teams—Nikhil and Victor versus a couple of girls from Amanda's Blue bunk—and they were standing so far apart that you could fit a school bus between them.

"Throw!" said a counselor. One girl tossed the balloon up, and the other fumbled it. It fell, but it didn't break, causing the Blue team to clap and holler. At the same time, Nikhil lobbed the balloon up and across to Victor. It was too light a throw, and Victor had to run up a few feet, but he stretched out his arms and caught it, gently cradling it in his hands so it didn't break. The Green team erupted into cheers.

"They're unstoppable!" shouted Gabe, holding up his hands for a double high-five.

"Go, Nikhil!" Wesley shouted, slapping them. He had dropped their balloon before the game had even begun, but the sun was so hot that his shorts were already almost dry.

The counselors went around and made sure all the players took equal steps back. They were practically at opposite ends of the field. "Ready . . . throw!"

But before Nikhil could throw, a whizzing noise sounded

from near the classrooms. "Heads up!" someone yelled.

Something was falling from the sky, spinning out of control. Gabe covered his head and ran toward the perimeter of the field with the other screaming campers. The object landed with a *pop*—right on the trash bag of loaded water balloons for that afternoon.

The bag's contents shot into the air in a colorful geyser of water and latex. Some balloons shot up whole and then popped when they landed on the ground, splattering anyone in the vicinity. After the explosion, the crowd stood looking at one another, silent and soaking. Nikhil stared forlornly at the mess. He'd sacrificed his water balloon to save himself, and it was impossible to even identify it among the hundreds of casualties.

The counselors went to investigate the point of impact. Whatever had landed was trapped inside the trash bag, which lay shriveled on the ground with water leaking from all sides.

The Rocket Science instructor came running from the science building. She was wearing a lab coat and boxy goggles over her large glasses. "Sorry to bother you," she said, trying to catch her breath. "But has anyone seen a rocket? I was testing rockets for class on Monday, and I seem to have added too much calcium carbide." Only then did she notice the group of counselors huddled around the soggy trash bag. "Ah! I think that's it!"

Everyone started laughing and talking. Nikhil apologized repeatedly to Victor, even though their Blue competitors had lost their balloon too. Gabe stared wide-eyed at the scene, shocked that something as regular as field day could be interrupted by something as smart as rocket science. So much for Color War filling the left side of his chart without qualifiers on the right. But then he saw something that made him forget about his logic proof altogether. It was Amanda, and she was waddling toward him with her T-shirt and shorts plastered to her skin. Her hair was hanging in long, wet pieces. A broken red water balloon sat atop her head, its tie poking straight up.

"What?" she said.

Wesley and Nikhil laughed so hard that they fell on top of each other. Gabe laughed so hard, he started to cry.

"Everyone's wet," said Amanda. "It's not funny."

"No, it's not funny," he managed to say through heavy breaths. Amanda stood with her arms crossed, the water from her shorts dripping into a puddle underneath her. Gabe wheezed. "It's hilarious!"

Problem: Am I a nerd who only has nerdy adventures?

Hypothesis: No.

Proof:

THINGS I CAN TELL ZACK (I am not a nerd.)	THINGS I CAN'T TELL ZACK (I am a nerd.)
1. I'm going to sleepaway camp for six weeks!	1. It is the Summer Center for Gifted Enrichment.
2. My bunkmates are really cool, and we became friends right away!	2. They like learning digits of π.
3. The food is bad, just like at camps in ~~books and~~ movies!	3. We fixed it with lemon juice to kill the bacteria.
4. I'm being stalked by an annoying girl!	4. She is in my Logical Reasoning and Poetry Writing classes.
5. I creamed Amanda in a sing-off!	5. We sang all the countries of the world.
6. We put music and sports pictures on our walls.	6. They are of Beethoven and the rules of badminton.
7. Wesley says amazing things in his sleep!	7. He solves math problems. 7a. and brainteasers.
8. I tried some cool hairstyles that lots of girls said looked cute.	8. One is named for Julius Caesar.
9. Vampire lice are sucking the blood out of people's heads!	9. We learned all about the *Pediculus humanus capitis* and their life cycle.

169

THINGS I CAN TELL ZACK (I am not a nerd.)	THINGS I CAN'T TELL ZACK (I am a nerd.)
10. I discovered a top secret operation!	10. It was an operation to study the science of lice.
11. I hung out with the coolest guy at camp!	11. His nickname is C^2, and he is so smart, he skipped two grades.
12. Color War broke with aliens landing in the middle of the night!	12. Our algorithm was off by a few days.
13. Green won 90 points in field day!	13. A rocket crashed into the water-balloon toss because the teacher added too much calcium carbide.

Chapter 20

SCAVENGER HUNT STRATEGY

Dear Mom,

This is just a very short letter, because we're in the middle of Color War and it is so so so so SO much fun!! We are going to plan for the scavenger hunt now. Zack said you have a surprise for me when you come pick me up. What is it?

After a lunch of salad and pasta with green pesto, everyone had an hour of free time. But no one was going to use that time as free. The counselors weren't allowed to run Color

War stuff with their teams during free time, but C^2 was a part of Green Nation, and he called a meeting to plan their strategy for the scavenger hunt. The counselors handed out lists for the scavenger hunt at the end of lunch, but teams had until Sunday morning, the final day of Color War, to complete it.

"We'll get two hours on Sunday to do it," C^2 explained, "but if we wait until then, we don't stand a chance. If we want to win, we've got to start now."

Green wasn't the only team that was forging a scavenger hunt plan now. The Red team was huddled in the woods. Yellow was clumped on the pavement in front of the Humanities building. Blue was underneath the big tree on the edge of Shady Field. But having C^2 on their team meant Green had the best spot: the playground. C^2 himself was standing at the top of the slide, and everyone else was on the jungle gym. Gabe and Wesley had prime spots on top of the monkey bars. Nikhil, who preferred a seat he couldn't accidentally slip through, was sitting on the wood right by Gabe's dangling feet.

"I've looked through the list," C^2 continued. "It's a lot of stuff, but nothing impossible. Well . . ." He looked up at the sky, contemplating something. Deciding against whatever it was he was considering, he said, "Yeah, nothing impossible. So, here's the plan. I'm going to give each bunk a bunch of items from the list. You can find those items all together or you can split them up further. I don't care. But start working right away, okay? I'm going to come around to your bunks before lights out. If there's anything in your list you think you can't get, tell me by lights out *tonight*. Got it? Then bring everything you have so far to me by *tomorrow* night before lights out. That way, Sunday morning we can figure out as a whole team who can get the stuff that's missing, or how to be creative and make stuff that we can't get."

The boys from Gabe's bunk gathered underneath the monkey bars to look at the section of the list C^2 had assigned them. After some arguing about the most efficient way to tackle it, and then about how arguing was inefficient, they decided to split the list into smaller lists by number and then let sections of the bunk choose their list based on what they knew they could get.

Since Gabe knew about similes and metaphors from his Poetry Writing class, he claimed the first seven items for himself and Wesley and Nikhil.

1. A simile
2. A metaphor
3. A cup of red sand

4. Seaweed
5. The tenth word in the second column on page 237 of the *Concise Oxford English Dictionary*
6. A dime from 1996
7. A picture of someone on your team with a celebrity

The first two just required a bit of thought. The dime shouldn't be too hard; between them and everyone in their bunk, there was bound to be one from 1996. The sand and the seaweed they would probably get by the lake, which they'd be going to right after free time. Number five just involved going to the library and looking it up. They had fifteen minutes before they had to change for swimming, so they decided to walk over to the library now.

"I bet we could finish our whole part of the list by today," said Wesley.

"What about the picture of someone with a celebrity?" said Gabe. "Have you guys ever met a celebrity?"

"An author came to my school once," said Nikhil, "but I didn't get a picture with her."

"I went to SeaWorld and petted Shamu," said Wesley proudly. When he saw that his bunkmates weren't impressed, he added, "Shamu's a famous whale."

Gabe laughed. "Did you get a picture?"

"Yeah," said Wesley, "but I don't have it here. I *knew* I should have brought it."

"I don't know if that would work, anyway," said Nikhil as the boys entered the library. "The judges might not know it's Shamu."

"Yeah," said Gabe, "they might think we gave them a picture of you petting a not-famous whale."

They all laughed but then covered their mouths when the librarian signaled for them to be quiet. The three of them walked up to her desk.

Nikhil asked, "Where can we find the *Concise Oxford English Dictionary*?"

Wesley asked, "Where would I find a book about Shamu?"

Gabe and Nikhil followed the librarian's pointed finger to the window ledge, where a large, thick book lay open. Gabe needed to use both his hands to flip it closed. "*Concise Oxford English Dictionary*," he read. "What page?"

The dictionary was so big that the tenth word in the

second column of page 237 was only CENTURY. They were heft-
ing the book into the copy machine—Nikhil had suggested
they make a copy of the page for proof, just to be safe—when
Wesley showed up with a book about whales. He had the
book open to a big picture, spread over two pages, of a black-
and-white killer whale. The caption had a paragraph that said
something about Shamu and SeaWorld.

"Looks like the original Shamu died in 1971," said Wesley
with a sad sigh. "So, the Shamu I petted wasn't the really
famous one."

"It's still pretty famous, though," said Gabe. "We could
take a picture of you and this picture. Then we'd have a picture of you and a celebrity!"

"That's a good idea!" said Nikhil. "But it doesn't have to
be Shampoo."

"Shamu," Wesley corrected. "May she rest in peace."

"We could take a picture of one of us with a picture of a
real celebrity," Nikhil continued.

"Or," said Gabe, tapping his nose, "we could take a picture we have of one of us and then photocopy it with a picture of a celebrity, and then it'll look like they're the same
picture."

"Or go to the computer lab and scan them," said Wesley, forgetting that he was in mourning for Shamu.

"Oh, I know!" said Gabe. He remembered that C^2 had said something about being creative and making stuff they couldn't get. He realized, with a jolt of excitement, that this was the spirit of the scavenger hunt. "We could, like, get a girl counselor to put on big sunglasses and a hat and put her hand up like she doesn't want to be photographed, and then take a picture of her like that and one of us. It would totally look like we're with a celebrity."

"Is that cheating?" asked Nikhil.

"I don't think so," said Gabe. "It's like C^2 said. We should be creative."

"He said we'd be creative on Sunday morning, to make stuff nobody could get for real," Nikhil clarified. "First let's see if anyone in our bunk has a picture with a celebrity. That'd be easy and safe."

"We can ask people at swimming," said Wesley.

"Swimming!" said Nikhil with a start. "We'd better hurry up."

In the fifteen minutes the boys had spent in the library, the weather seemed to have forgotten that it was summer. Big blocks of clouds blanketed the sky in gray. The humid air dropped in temperature, and a rising wind cut along the top of the lake. It wasn't raining, so swim wasn't canceled, but the air was so cold that most of the kids chose to stand around on the dock wearing their towels like cloaks.

Nikhil called staying out of the water to look for dimes and celebrity photos. That meant Gabe and Wesley had to go in search of red sand and seaweed.

"You're brave," Amanda said to Gabe when she saw that he and Wesley were going in. Her towel was wrapped tightly around her whole body and head, so that only her face was visible.

Gabe rolled his eyes. "I hope we find this stuff quickly," he said to Wesley. He put on his prescription goggles.

"Me squared," said Wesley. He fastened his nose plug.

The two of them jumped off the dock.

"Yeeow!" shouted Wesley. "It's as cold as an ice age in here."

"That's a simile!" Gabe said. "We can use it for our list."

"Okay," said Wesley with a shiver. "Now let's get the other things and get out!"

Gabe dove deep underwater and looked for red sand

and seaweed. After a few minutes, he changed his goal to finding any color sand and any weed. He swam out to the floating dock. He swam back to the shore, where the water was lapping loudly against the rocks. But the floor of the lake had only mud, and the water was devoid of plant matter.

After ten minutes, the boys climbed back onto the dock and huddled in their towels. They didn't have any red sand or seaweed, only goosebumps and blue lips. They hurried over to Nikhil, who was standing where the dock met the shore.

"Did you find someone with a celebrity photo?" Gabe asked.

Nikhil shook his head.

"A 1996 dime?" asked Wesley.

Nikhil shook his head again.

And I thought we'd be done with our list by dinnertime today, Gabe thought. He had daydreamed about reporting to C^2 that there was nothing on their list they couldn't find— because they had it all already! Then C^2 would congratulate them and ask them to help him find a few items from his own list and, while he was at it, invite them to spend recess with him and his friends. Then Gabe would fill up the left column of his logic proof with all the cool stuff they did, and Modus Tollens would prove that he was not really a nerd.

Now Gabe felt stupid for even having imagined that. They only had three of their seven items, and it looked like the odds of finding the others were slim.

Jenny Chin, wearing her towel like a long, formfitting dress, waddled over to the boys and tapped Gabe on the shoulder. "I shouldn't even be talking to you because you're on Green and you're the enemy. But my brother told me to tell you that he wants to talk to you tonight when he comes around."

Instead of feeling elated at C^2's wanting to talk to him, Gabe felt miserable. There went their chance at not talking to C^2 until the next night, when they might have figured out how to get some of their missing items. "How come?" he asked.

Jenny shrugged and waddled away.

"He's not coming around until after activities," Gabe said in an effort to reassure his bunkmates and himself. "Let's try to at least get one more thing by then."

Problem: Am I a nerd who only has nerdy adventures?

Hypothesis: No.

Proof:

THINGS I CAN TELL ZACK (I am not a nerd.)	THINGS I CAN'T TELL ZACK (I am a nerd.)
1. I'm going to sleepaway camp for six weeks!	1. It is the Summer Center for Gifted Enrichment.
2. My bunkmates are really cool, and we became friends right away!	2. They like learning digits of π.
3. The food is bad, just like at camps in ~~books and~~ movies!	3. We fixed it with lemon juice to kill the bacteria.
4. I'm being stalked by an annoying girl!	4. She is in my Logical Reasoning and Poetry Writing classes.
5. I creamed Amanda in a sing-off!	5. We sang all the countries of the world.
6. We put music and sports pictures on our walls.	6. They are of Beethoven and the rules of badminton.
7. Wesley says amazing things in his sleep!	7. He solves math problems. 7a. and brainteasers.
8. I tried some cool hairstyles that lots of girls said looked cute.	8. One is named for Julius Caesar.
9. Vampire lice are sucking the blood out of people's heads!	9. We learned all about the *Pediculus humanus capitis* and their life cycle.

THINGS I CAN TELL ZACK (I am not a nerd.)	THINGS I CAN'T TELL ZACK (I am a nerd.)
10. I discovered a top secret operation!	10. It was an operation to study the science of lice.
11. I hung out with the coolest guy at camp!	11. His nickname is C^2, and he is so smart, he skipped two grades.
12. Color War broke with aliens landing in the middle of the night!	12. Our algorithm was off by a few days.
13. Green won 90 points in field day!	13. A rocket crashed into the water-balloon toss because the teacher added too much calcium carbide.
14. We got three of our scavenger hunt items.	14. They are a simile, a metaphor, and a word from the dictionary.

Chapter 21

THE FIRST BIT OF LUCK

Their first piece of good luck happened during dinner (hot dogs with color-coded toppings: mustard, ketchup, relish, and dyed-blue sauerkraut). Word spread that one of the Red team members had an extra 1996 dime and that he would sell it to another team for the right price. Gabe and his bunkmates went over to his table.

"Yeah, I've got a 1996 dime. What's it worth?" the Red team kid asked.

"It's a dime," said Wesley. "So it's worth ten cents." He laughed.

The boy rolled his eyes. "What's it worth to *you*? I'm not selling it for ten cents."

"A pack of Twizzlers?" Gabe asked.

The boy considered. "I heard you guys got the dictionary word already. Twizzlers, the dictionary word, and a metaphor, and you've got a deal."

"No way!" said Nikhil. "We're not trading two items for one *and* giving you Twizzlers."

"Yeah," said Wesley. "Forget it." He stood up to walk away.

"All right," said the Red kid. "Just the dictionary word and the metaphor, then."

Gabe narrowed his eyes. The dictionary word could be looked up easily, so Red was bound to find it whether they gave it to them or not. But a metaphor was harder—even some of the people in Poetry Writing had trouble writing metaphors, and the one Gabe had come up with, "The atmosphere blankets the earth," was too good to just give away. "Just the dictionary word," he said firmly. "You have to find your own metaphor."

The boy chewed on this along with his ketchup-covered hot dog. "I'm going to check to make sure it's the right word," he said between bites.

Gabe tried not to smile. If the Red team looked up the word to check it, it would be the same as looking up the word to find it. He glanced at his bunkmates and saw that they were thinking the same thing. "It'll be the right word," he promised. "Deal?"

They went back to their table with one more item from their list complete.

Chapter 22

THE SECOND BIT OF LUCK

Gabe would have been satisfied with only having the four successes to report to C^2. But instead of homework and activities, the whole camp was going to the theater to compete in Color War *Jeopardy!* And that was when they had their second bit of luck—and a surprise that was just as exciting as when Color War broke.

Following the counselors, the campers marched into the theater and filed into seats. Streamers of different colors were strung between the seats to demarcate where each team was meant to sit. The curtain was drawn across the stage.

Once everyone was seated, the counselors ran up onto the stage in front of the curtain.

"Is everyone ready for *Jeopardy!?*" one of them shouted.

Everyone nodded. A few people clapped. One kid in the back said, "Yeah!"

The counselor put her hands on her hips. "I can't hear you!" she yelled. "I *said*, IS EVERYONE READY FOR *JEOPARDY!?*"

This time, everyone clapped and whistled and stomped and roared.

"That's more like it!" she cried. "Here we go!"

The *Jeopardy!* theme song came blasting over the speakers as the curtain opened. Everyone sang along and then broke into applause again. It was a real *Jeopardy!* set—podiums, buzzers, a tower of blue screens, and all!

The theme song ended, and the camp director's voice took its place. "Welcome to SCGE Color War *Jeopardy!* Here's your host, Alex Trebek!"

And then the most incredible thing happened. Alex Trebek came walking out onto the stage. The whole theater erupted into cheers.

"That's Alex Trebek!" Gabe screamed. "The real guy from TV!"

"Maybe it just looks like him," said Nikhil, but his voice betrayed his excitement.

"No, that's Alex Trebek!" squealed Wesley. "Do you see him? That's really him."

Gabe had heard that once or twice in the past, a celebrity showed up to break Color War. But Color War had already broken. Having the actual host of *Jeopardy!* for their game was an amazing bonus.

With such large teams, each person only got to stand at the podium and attempt to answer one question per round. Green Nation did well until Double *Jeopardy!*, when a whole string of Red players knew U.S. presidents the way Gabe and his bunkmates knew digits of Pi.

For Final *Jeopardy!*, each team was allowed to come up with an answer as a group. The category "Native Species" had Green confident enough to wager more than half of their points. If they got it right and Red got it wrong, they could move up to first place.

The whole theater was silent as Alex read the clue.

"Native to this region but rarely seen at Summer Center, this harmless snake has red blotches and a name that belongs in your breakfast cereal."

The clue was accompanied by a picture of a long, tan snake with big red blotches. Each blotch was outlined in black, like it came right out of a coloring book. Even though the clue said the snake was harmless, some people couldn't help but gasp at the sight of the photo.

The Green team, bunched up and anxious, whispered frantically while the *Jeopardy!* theme song played.

"Is that a garter snake?"

"No, those are brown."

"I held a boa constrictor once."

"Don't you know all about snakes?"

"No, I know all about lizards."

"Quiet!" said C². "Does anyone know the answer for sure?"

No one spoke.

"What about that breakfast cereal thing," said Gabe. "What does that mean?"

"This harmless snake has a name that belongs in your breakfast cereal," Wesley read.

"Raisin snake?" guessed one girl. "A lot of cereals have raisins."

"Lemon juice snake, if it might have bacteria," mumbled Nikhil.

"Spoon snake!" said someone else. "You eat cereal with a spoon!"

What is it? Gabe thought. *What is it?*

The song was coming to a close, and the team had to write

down an answer. In the last few seconds, another girl said, "Do raisin snake. Those red spots can kind of look like raisins."

C^2 scribbled down "What is Raisin Snake?" just as the music hit its final note. Everyone waited for the correct answer, but only the Blue team looked happy.

The Yellow team wrongly guessed King Cobra, and their score dropped dramatically. Gabe wasn't too surprised when Raisin Snake was wrong too. Now they had to hope Blue and Red got it wrong and had wagered a lot. Blue's answer was Red Spotted Snake, which was also wrong—but they were still happy, because they'd wagered nothing. That left them in second place behind Red.

"Red Nation," said Alex, "let's see your response."

They held up their card. It read, WHAT IS MILK SNAKE?

"Milk snake," said Alex, "or, native to this region, eastern milk snake, is correct! Let's see what you wagered."

It didn't matter what Red had wagered—it was clear that they'd won.

Disappointed at the outcome but still enthralled by the spectacle of the whole event, all the campers lined up to get Alex Trebek's autograph.

"Milk snake," said Wesley. "Why didn't we think of that?"

"I know," said Gabe. "Cereal and milk—it's so obvious."

Nikhil motioned for the camp director to come over. "Are there really eastern milk snakes in this area?" he asked gravely.

The director shrugged. "They're native to this region, yes, but no one's ever seen one in my time here, and that's going on twenty years. But even if you did, they look scary, but they're one hundred percent harmless."

"You're sure?" Nikhil asked. Just to be safe.

The director patted his shoulder. "Positive."

"We can't find our scavenger hunt stuff, and now we lose this," said Wesley. "I can't believe they knew the eastern milk snake."

"Now I'll know it forever," said Gabe, looking at the photo of the snake on the big screen.

"We're not out of luck in the scavenger hunt!" Nikhil realized, forgetting the snake. "Let's ask David to take a picture of us with Alex Trebek—a photo of teammates with a real celebrity!"

Their high spirits restored, they got the host's autograph and took a photo. Wesley, beaming, said, "This is even better than meeting Shamu."

Alex Trebek raised his eyebrows and said, "Thank you."

Problem: Am I a nerd who only has nerdy adventures?

Hypothesis: No.

Proof:

THINGS I CAN TELL ZACK (I am not a nerd.)	THINGS I CAN'T TELL ZACK (I am a nerd.)
1. I'm going to sleepaway camp for six weeks!	1. It is the Summer Center for Gifted Enrichment.
2. My bunkmates are really cool, and we became friends right away!	2. They like learning digits of π.
3. The food is bad, just like at camps in ~~books and~~ movies!	3. We fixed it with lemon juice to kill the bacteria.
4. I'm being stalked by an annoying girl!	4. She is in my Logical Reasoning and Poetry Writing classes.
5. I creamed Amanda in a sing-off!	5. We sang all the countries of the world.
6. We put music and sports pictures on our walls.	6. They are of Beethoven and the rules of badminton.
7. Wesley says amazing things in his sleep!	7. He solves math problems. 7a. and brainteasers.
8. I tried some cool hairstyles that lots of girls said looked cute.	8. One is named for Julius Caesar.
9. Vampire lice are sucking the blood out of people's heads!	9. We learned all about the *Pediculus humanus capitis* and their life cycle.

THINGS I CAN TELL ZACK (I am not a nerd.)	THINGS I CAN'T TELL ZACK (I am a nerd.)
10. I discovered a top secret operation!	10. It was an operation to study the science of lice.
11. I hung out with the coolest guy at camp!	11. His nickname is C^2, and he is so smart, he skipped two grades.
12. Color War broke with aliens landing in the middle of the night!	12. Our algorithm was off by a few days.
13. Green won 90 points in field day!	13. A rocket crashed into the water-balloon toss because the teacher added too much calcium carbide.
14. We got ~~three~~ five of our scavenger hunt items.	14. They ~~are~~ include a simile, a metaphor, and a word from the dictionary.
15. A celebrity came to camp, and I got a picture with him!	15. He's the host of a game show for smart people.

Chapter 23

THE THIRD BIT OF LUCK

Their third bit of luck came when they were back in their cabin after *Jeopardy!*

Wesley sang, "We are the champions, my friends!" He continued in the same tune but with his own words. "We found almost everything for the hu-unt! We are the champions, the scavenger hunt champions, we are the champions of caaaamp!" When he tried to hit the high note, his voice cracked, and Gabe and Nikhil burst out laughing.

"Thank you, thank you," Wesley said, bowing. "That was 'We Are the Scavenger Hunt Champions,' written and performed by Wesley Fan, Scavenger Hunt Champion."

"Well, we're not scavenger hunt champions *yet*," Nikhil reminded them. "We still need to find seaweed and red sand."

"Still," said Gabe. "We can tell C^2 that we have five out of our seven."

"That is really good," Nikhil admitted. "Five out of seven is, like"—he did some mental calculations—"five sevenths."

Gabe and Wesley cracked up again, and Gabe wrote that quote on their Funny Quotes poster, right below the question Wesley had asked during lunch the week before: "Which would you rather be: a marsupial or a porpoise?"

"I think," said Wesley, "that we deserve a reward for being scavenger hunt champions." He stood on Gabe's mattress, reached up to the top bunk, and wedged his hand between his mattress and bed frame.

"What are you doing?" Gabe asked.

"My mom mailed me my all-time favorite snack a few weeks ago, but I was saving it till the very end of camp."

"You've been sleeping on it for a few *weeks*? It's probably totally flattened."

"That's okay. It's supposed to be flat." Wesley lifted the mattress up, pulled it toward himself, and balanced it on his head. Then he felt around the opening until he found what he was looking for. He jumped down from Gabe's bed holding out three long, flat sheets of plastic. "Ta da!" he said. He gave Gabe and Nikhil their own sheets before ripping one open himself and taking a bite.

Gabe turned his over in his hands. There was lots of writing on the package, but it was all in what looked to be Japanese. He ripped open the top and slid out the contents. It looked kind of like a dark Fruit Rollup, only less sticky and much, much thinner—it was so thin, Gabe could almost see through it. "What is it?" he asked finally.

"*Nori*," said Wesley. "We get it at the Asian supermarket. It's so good."

Nori, Gabe thought. He closed his eyes, held the sheet up to his nose, and sniffed. It smelled like something he knew he'd smelled before, only he couldn't quite place it. "But what is it?" he asked. "Like, what's it made of?"

"It kind of smells like fish," said Nikhil.

"Yeah, because it's . . . what do you call it. . . ." Wesley thought. "It's not fish, but it's from the ocean. But it's dried. You use it to wrap sushi. It's like, you know, that green stuff that floats in the ocean."

"Seaweed?" said Gabe.

"Yeah! It's dried seaweed. Try it. It's so good."

Nikhil shouted, "Seaweed! We need seaweed for the scavenger hunt!"

Gabe said, "And you've had it under your bed this whole time!"

Wesley's eyes widened and his mouth opened as he put together the pieces. "Oh, yeah. I am the ultimate scavenger hunt champion."

"Don't sing," said Nikhil.

Someone knocked on the wall that divided their section of the cabin from the next. It was C^2, for real, in their bunk. Gabe had thought he'd looked cool that day in the lice lab when he was wearing a shower cap, but he looked impossibly cool now in a white T-shirt, green hospital scrubs for pants, and a pair of khaki flip-flops. His black hair was cut short around his face, but in the center of his head a few strands from each side were gelled toward one another, forming a tent shape on the top of his head. It was a hairstyle Gabe had tried, but he didn't remember it looking as slick. Gabe thought that, as far as camp went, if they hadn't managed to get a picture with Alex Trebek, a picture with C^2 would probably have counted.

"What's that about being an ultimate scavenger hunt champion?" he asked.

"We all are," said Gabe. "We already have six out of the seven things on our list."

"As Nikhil would say," said Wesley, "that's, like, six sevenths." Nikhil shot him a look of death, and Wesley stopped laughing and added, "Just kidding."

Gabe said, "We're only missing—"

C^2 finished his sentence for him: "Red sand."

Gabe wondered how he knew. Jenny couldn't have told him; they'd only just found the seaweed a minute ago. The mysterious way he seemed to know everything without even trying only added to his allure.

Gabe said, "Yeah. I was thinking that if we can't find any red sand, then we could get some regular sand and dye it red somehow."

C^2 shook his head as if to say, *Amateurs.* "Where are you going to get regular sand? The lake only has mud on the bottom."

"Maybe mixed in the dirt on the playground . . . ," Nikhil wondered aloud.

C^2 shook his head again. "Here's the deal. Red sand has

been on the scavenger hunt list every year. The past few years it was easy because Sand Art was a choice for activities one night. So you just had to go in the arts and crafts closet and steal some. But this year there was no Sand Art. And there's no sand in the arts and crafts closet. I checked."

"So what do we do?" Gabe asked. "How do we get it?"

"There is one place that has red sand. But you know why the sand is red there."

Gabe felt goose bumps rising on his skin. He had a feeling he knew what C² was going to say. "Where?" he asked.

C² looked him straight in the eye. "Dead Man's Island."

Problem: Am I a nerd who only has nerdy adventures?

Hypothesis: No.

Proof:

THINGS I CAN TELL ZACK (I am not a nerd.)	THINGS I CAN'T TELL ZACK (I am a nerd.)
1. I'm going to sleepaway camp for six weeks!	1. It is the Summer Center for Gifted Enrichment.
2. My bunkmates are really cool, and we became friends right away!	2. They like learning digits of π.

THINGS I CAN TELL ZACK
(I am not a nerd.)

3. The food is bad, just like at camps in ~~books and~~ movies!

4. I'm being stalked by an annoying girl!

5. I creamed Amanda in a sing-off!

6. We put music and sports pictures on our walls.

7. Wesley says amazing things in his sleep!

8. I tried some cool hairstyles that lots of girls said looked cute.

9. Vampire lice are sucking the blood out of people's heads!

10. I discovered a top secret operation!

11. I hung out with the coolest guy at camp!

12. Color War broke with aliens landing in the middle of the night!

13. Green won 90 points in field day!

THINGS I CAN'T TELL ZACK
(I am a nerd.)

3. We fixed it with lemon juice to kill the bacteria.

4. She is in my Logical Reasoning and Poetry Writing classes.

5. We sang all the countries of the world.

6. They are of Beethoven and the rules of badminton.

7. He solves math problems.
7a. and brainteasers.

8. One is named for Julius Caesar.

9. We learned all about the *Pediculus humanus capitis* and their life cycle.

10. It was an operation to study the science of lice.

11. His nickname is C^2, and he is so smart, he skipped two grades.

12. Our algorithm was off by a few days.

13. A rocket crashed into the water-balloon toss because the teacher added too much calcium carbide.

THINGS I CAN TELL ZACK (I am not a nerd.)	THINGS I CAN'T TELL ZACK (I am a nerd.)
14. We got ~~three~~ ~~five~~ six of our scavenger hunt items.	14. They ~~are~~ include a simile, a metaphor, and a word from the dictionary.
15. A celebrity came to camp, and I got a picture with him!	15. He's the host of a game show for smart people.
16. I'm going to kayak to Dead Man's Island in the middle of the night.	

Chapter 24

DEAD MAN'S ISLAND

Dear Zack,

Tonight I'm going to kayak to Dead Man's Island. Here's why it's called Dead Man's Island. Two hundred years ago, two explorers canoed to Dead Man's Island together to collect samples. But when they got there, one of them murdered the other and left the body there! When he started to canoe back, the ghost of the dead man haunted the area around the island and made him lose his way. A few days later, an empty canoe came to the shore. The sand on Dead Man's Island is red because of the dead man's blood!

Now get this. I am going to kayak there by myself in the middle of the night to collect red sand for Color War.

Gabe had woken up so early, he finished writing to Zack before the siren even went off. The air was cool and crisp, and a wavy patch of orange light shone through the bottom of the window. He reread the first line of his letter: Tonight I'm going to kayak to Dead Man's Island.

He didn't have to. He could back out. Like Nikhil said, it was just one item in a long scavenger hunt list, and chances were no other team would have it, either. Or he could let C² or another older kid go. C² had offered. But Gabe had said he would do it. And he'd said it with such surety. He hadn't even flinched. At least, he hoped he hadn't.

It's just kayaking, he thought. But it wasn't just kayaking. It was kayaking by himself in the middle of the night, in the pitch black, to somewhere he had never been and wasn't supposed to go. Somewhere that was haunted. C² had given him a map and a compass. But there wouldn't be any lifeguards on the dock watching and ready to jump in and save him. And there wouldn't be any counselor to count up the kids and notice that he hadn't come back.

According to the map, Dead Man's Island was small and perfectly circular. It was just around the bend in the lake, through a narrow inlet that was hidden by clumps of trees that hung over the water, and just beyond a round area marked Lily Pad Lagoon.

Gabe didn't think the legend could be true, and he didn't think he believed in ghosts. But he also didn't think he wanted to kayak there alone at night and find out.

But there was no other way to do it. He couldn't go during the day, because he had the water sports competition instead of regular swim time. And anyway, he'd get in trouble if he tried to go with lifeguards watching, since you were only allowed to kayak in the marked area. That was also why he couldn't go during free time: The lifeguards would be there. The only time was after lights out. And there was no one to go with him. Nikhil was good at kayaking, but there was no way he'd even consider something as unsafe as this. Wesley would love to go, but he was terrible at kayaking. C^2 or one of the older kids could go with him, but that would mean admitting he was too scared to go alone. A couple of other boys from his bunk had offered too, but the more Gabe thought about it, the more he felt that he needed to tackle this alone. Of course he was scared. But why? He'd just go there, get a cup of red sand, and come back. No need to even get out of the kayak.

Above him, Wesley wiggled onto his side and hugged the inside of his sleeping bag. He murmured, "You can do it."

Gabe nodded. *I can* do it, he thought. *Zack will think I'm so cool.* He had to; there was nothing geeky about an adventure like this. He'd be going back to the noncamp world soon, becoming Zack's brother for real, and he wanted to fit in in his new family.

And here at camp, kayaking to Dead Man's Island would make him a hero on his team, and it would impress C^2. He knew what Zack would think of C^2—C^2 had skipped two grades and thought science was fun. But he wondered what C^2 would think of Zack. Gabe wouldn't want C^2 to see Zack's letters, that much was sure. He didn't know whose opinion was right—or whose he should care about more.

Well, he thought, *kayaking to Dead Man's Island will impress them both.*

The silence of the morning was cut by the blare of the wake-up siren, and the boys began to stir. Ready or not, today was the day.

Chapter 25

FRICTION COEFFICIENT

It was the second day of Color War, and the competitive spirit of the camp was fired up. Gabe's counselor passed some tubes of green face paint around the bunk, and the boys applied it like war paint. Gabe put lines under his eyes like a football player would do. Nikhil wrote GREEN on his left arm and NATION on his right. When Wesley returned after ten minutes in the bathroom, he had a big symbol on his whole face. "That's cool," said Nikhil. "What is it?"

"Duh," said Wesley. "It's a *G*."

Gabe cocked his head. "Did you do it in the mirror?" he asked.

"Yeah, why?"

He cracked up. "Because it's backward!"

At breakfast the director of the camp read out the current standings.

"In fourth place," she shouted, "is the YELLOW TEAM with 90 points!"

Yellow broke into applause, but the other three teams cheered even louder because if yellow was in last place, it meant that they weren't.

"In third place," she called, "is the GREEN TEAM with 145 points!"

Red and Blue cheered the loudest now, and Green clapped. Some girls from one of the Green bunks started chanting, "That's all right, that's okay, we're gonna beat you anyway!" The rest of Green joined in, but the director quieted them down after two rounds.

"In second place," she announced, "with 160 points, is the BLUE TEAM!"

"We're only 15 points behind," said Nikhil excitedly. "One win in water sports or the obstacle course and we'll move up."

"Or one item they don't have on the scavenger hunt," said Wesley. "Like red sand."

Gabe nodded stoically.

"And in FIRST PLACE," the director said, even though she could barely be heard above the talking, "with 205 points . . . is the RED TEAM!"

Red broke into a rousing rendition of "We're Red, we rock," and the other teams clapped politely. Then Yellow began chanting, "Go Red, you rock!" in an obvious effort to snag the 200 points for sportsmanship that were still up for grabs.

The director reminded them that today's battles were worth a total of 800 points, and tomorrow the scavenger hunt was worth another 400. "Add team spirit and sportsmanship for 200 each," she said, "and it's still very much anyone's game. So, eat a big breakfast and get ready to give it your all today."

Between the amped-up atmosphere and the superfun battles, Gabe could almost forget what he was going to do that night.

The first battle was the obstacle course, which was rumored to always be one of the best parts of Color War. It absolutely lived up to expectations. First you had to jump through a line of tires. Then you had to solve three arithmetic problems—inside a smelly port-a-potty. After that you had to run with an egg on a spoon across the field, and dropping the egg cost your team points. After depositing the egg in your team's color-coded bin, you came to a huge map of the world on the ground, and you had to locate the country or body of water that the counselor called out. From there, you slid down a giant inflatable slide into a mud pit. Once you used the mud as paint to correctly spell a word on a wall, you were done.

The counselors had to do it too, as did the teachers, and even the director and the nurse. Miss Carey screamed as she went down the slide, and Mr. Justice dunked his whole body in the mud pool and emerged with long, dripping dreadlocks of mud. By the end of the morning, the entire camp was a walking, grinning gloopy brown mess.

The younger kids had water sports in the afternoon, and Gabe did everything he could to rack up points for Green. While he was standing on the dock, wearing his towel still and getting ready to compete in the first race, he had a moment of panic and thought that maybe he shouldn't be doing *every-thing* he could to win—maybe he shouldn't be wearing what he was wearing under his towel. After all, this wasn't a regular swim meet, where everyone was representing a swim team.

Gabe removed his glasses and handed them to the life-guard. Then he shifted his prescription goggles from his forehead onto his face, and the lake once again came into focus. He saw the other swimmers drop their towels and toss them behind themselves. They were all wearing the type of bathing suit Gabe usually wore to swim in the lake: knee-length and baggy with cargo pockets on either side. *Too late to change now*, he thought. He removed his towel to reveal his suit: a tiny, tight-fitting Speedo.

He heard the crowd behind him gasp. He could hear some of the boys laughing and could sense the girls pointing. He didn't even want to think about Amanda's reaction. But he could also see that his competitors were nervous. They knew he meant business.

"No fair," complained the Red swimmer. "He's got so much less friction."

"Yeah," said Yellow. "His friction coefficient is probably, like, point zero five."

"On your mark!" shouted the lifeguard.

Gabe moved to the edge of the dock, bent over, and assumed a launching position. The other swimmers did the same, following his lead.

"Get set!"

Gabe lifted his butt into the air. He didn't even hear the

snickers behind him or the person who said, "I see Green team's underpants!" He was in the zone.

"GO!"

Gabe catapulted off the dock and cut swiftly through the water. The other swimmers didn't stand a chance. He tagged the floating island and swam back to the dock almost twice as quickly as the second-place finisher from Blue. The Green team went crazy. A bunch of his bunkmates rushed toward him to pat him on the back or hug him or lift him onto their shoulders, but they stopped a few feet away once they remembered the Speedo. Still, Gabe thought, *I'll be a hero[2] after tonight.*

Chapter 26

THE LATE-NIGHT VOYAGE

Word got around that Gabe was planning on kayaking to Dead Man's Island, and between battles and meals, kids from the team kept giving him items they thought would help him prepare. He found a pair of binoculars on his bed after breakfast. After lunch, a few of his bunkmates gave him a flashlight and a roll of duct tape so he could attach the flashlight to his hat. And, during free time, he found an envelope with an anonymous note that said its contents would help ward off evil spirits. Gabe opened the envelope but then quickly closed it without even looking inside—whatever was in there smelled horrible.

But mostly people gave him things to read. Victor gave him an article from *National Geographic Kids* about what causes rapids, which was informative. Jenny brought him a book of ghost stories with a Post-it on the page where a ship of ghost pirates attack a boat of fishermen, which wasn't very helpful. Wesley lent him a battered copy of *The Adventures of Huckleberry Finn*, since Huck rafts down the river. Nikhil went to the library and took out *The Cay* and *Island of the Blue Dolphins*, just in case Gabe got stranded on the island and had to live off the land. Gabe thought he'd prepare better by rereading *Swallows and Amazons*—which had a sea-island adventure that *didn't* involve getting stranded or nearly dying—but when he discovered that neither of his bunkmates had read it, he insisted they read it immediately and gave them his copy.

The day went so quickly that he wouldn't have had time to read most of these materials anyway. After dinner, it was time to rehearse for the sing-off and then perform. Green wrote and sang "Green Will Rock You," a song to the tune of "We Will Rock You," which consisted of that one line repeated in all eleven languages spoken on the team. They thought they were better than Blue, who prefaced their song with a long explanation of why the sky is blue. Red was pretty impressive: They ended their song with not just a human pyramid, but also with a human trapezoid and even a human rhombus, and only one person fell. But it was Yellow that came from behind with what was undoubtedly the crowd favorite. They dressed up as robots and computers and sang their entire song in binary.

Before long, it was time for everyone to go back to the bunks. And shortly after that, it was lights out. And fifteen minutes after lights out, it was time for Gabe to go.

"Are you really going?" Nikhil said in the dark.

"Yeah," said Gabe. He was antsy with readiness and fear, and he hoped his voice betrayed only the former.

"Wear a life jacket," Nikhil said. "And the flashlight hat."

"Don't forget to bring back the sand," added Wesley with a silly snicker.

"Okay," said Gabe.

"Wake me up when you get back," said Nikhil.

"Okay," said Gabe. They sat for a few seconds in silence. Then he said, "Well, I'd better go before David gets back."

He unzipped his sleeping bag and peeled back the upper half, then slid his legs onto the floor and sat up. As he tiptoed down the aisle between bunks, boys whispered phrases of encouragement and, in case he didn't return, final words.

The cabin door was creaky, so he opened it just enough to slip out. The night was quiet, still, and cold. Apart from the low din of cicadas and the occasional voice from the clearing, where the counselors were hanging out, all Gabe could hear were his own footsteps. He walked in the dark until he was sure the cabin would block a view of him from the clearing. Only when he felt the turf of the field beneath him did he turn on the flashlight on his hat, cupping his hand across the top of it to keep the light from scattering. He quickly pointed it across the field to make sure he was heading in the right direction. *Ha*, he thought. *I'm* heading *in the right direction, and the flashlight is on my* head.

For some reason, this stupid joke gave him the confidence he needed to run to the lake. "One . . . ," he whispered to himself. He switched off the flashlight. "Two . . ." He took a breath. "Three!" Gabe exploded across the field like soda from a shaken can, and he didn't stop until he'd rounded the upper cabins, zoomed through the wooded path, and reached the lake. A few kayaks and paddles were lying upside down on the grass right by the water.

That was a relief; he wouldn't have to go into the shed and lug one out by himself, which would be difficult and noisy. He did go to the shed to get himself a life jacket, though— he was a strong swimmer, but he wasn't taking any risks for this trip. Besides, if something did happen to him and his body washed up on shore without a life jacket, what would Nikhil think of him?

He kicked off his sandals and dragged a kayak to the lake. It slid into the water with a low *plop*, and Gabe looked around to make sure no one had heard. He also worried, illogically, that someone might hear his heart pounding as he waded into the cold water and clambered into the kayak. But then he was in, and no one had come running from the campground, ready to bust him for breaking the rules. It was pitch black and stock silent and deathly *cold*. But a sudden rush of adrenaline sent blood pumping through Gabe's body. *I'm doing it!*

He took off with long, powerful strokes. He paddled out past the floating rope that marked the official kayaking zone, then aimed the kayak to the right. As he rounded the bend, his mind shifted to thoughts of going home. First he thought, *Nothing nerdy had better happen to cancel out this adventure.* But then, as the water became rougher and his strokes became stronger, he thought, *Why do I keep thinking so much about Zack?* He reached a part where he had to paddle through some trees, and he thought, *C^2 would think this is cool even if something geeky—*

There was a rustling in the leaves. Gabe pushed forward with his paddle to slow the kayak and stop in place. He shut off his flashlight and listened. The rustling noise came again. *It's probably just the wind*, Gabe thought. But he dipped his finger in the water and held it up. The air was completely still.

Swwwwwoooooooshshsh. The leaves rustled again, followed by a faint whimper. Gabe's whole body turned to ice. He felt his arm hairs stand at attention. There was something there. *It's the ghost*, he thought. He kept his eyes wide open behind his glasses, too afraid of heightening his other senses to even blink.

The rustling became louder, and the whimper turned into words. "Go away," the ghost moaned.

It doesn't want me to pass, Gabe thought. That was enough of a reason for him to turn back. He wanted to turn back. If only his brain would send the message to the motor axons to make the muscles in his arms put the paddle in the water and turn around. The breakdown in neural communication left him frozen and floating in place.

The leaves were moving now. They cut back and forth through the water with force. A sudden burst of light flashed from behind the leaves. Gabe choked on his scream, but the ghost's pierced the night. There was a high-pitched shriek, and then a cry of anguish: "NO!"

Gabe's respiratory system kicked in, and he started breathing again. That scream, that voice—it couldn't be from a ghost. It was too present and human and . . . familiar. Then his circulatory system kicked in, and he flicked on his flashlight.

The trees became silent and still. Now the ghost was afraid of *him*.

"Hello?" Gabe said.

There was no answer for a second. Then the voice came again: "Gabe?"

Gabe nearly fell out of his kayak. *"Amanda?"* he said.

"Gabe!" cried Amanda. "Thank God you followed me! My kayak is stuck in the branches, and my flashlight fell into the water."

Gabe let out a loud sigh. Never in his life did he think he'd be so happy to see Amanda Wisznewski. He paddled into the inlet until the nose of his kayak bumped the back of hers. "What are you doing here?" he asked as he moved his head around to scan the light over the water and find the branches that had caught her.

"Going to Dead Man's Island to get a cup of red sand. What are *you* doing here?"

Gabe laughed. "Going to Dead Man's Island to get a cup of red sand," he admitted. He might as well say it before she did. "Copying you."

Their relief made them laugh harder than the joke warranted.

Gabe pulled up through the dense leaves so that he was alongside Amanda. Then he pushed off her kayak and shined his hat beneath it. She had paddled into a tangle of branches, and they came to a thick knot right at the pointy part of the bottom of her boat. "You aren't afraid of the ghosts?" he asked.

"I was when you put on your flashlight!" she said. "*Man,* that was scary. I thought you were the ghost of the dead explorer."

"I wasn't as scary as *you*! The leaves were moving, and you were making noise. Why did you say 'go away'?"

"I was talking to the branches. They were everywhere!"

Gabe used the edge of his paddle to push the knot of branches down. "Try to go forward," he said.

Amanda pushed off Gabe's kayak and propelled herself forward. "Yes!" she said.

"Uh-oh," said Gabe. When Amanda had moved out of the trap, he had drifted in. Now his kayak was stuck.

Amanda turned to the side. "Here," she said. "Give me your paddle and I'll pull you."

Gabe stuck his paddle out to her and gripped the end. She reached the other end and pulled with all her might. At first it seemed like she was only going to pull herself back into the trees, but then she grabbed onto a branch with her other hand to hold her boat in place. With a jerk, Gabe's kayak became dislodged, and he drifted forward to meet her.

Once they were both through, Gabe moved his head in sweeping strokes to illuminate the area. "Wow," he whispered. It was Lily Pad Lagoon, and it was unbelievable. The water was low and perfectly calm. Large, flat lily pads dotted the surface, creating a floating, abstract checkerboard. Above them, sweeping tree branches arched around the perimeter in a dramatic canopy. Where the branches stopped, stars filled their place—hundreds of them, glowing like Christmas lights in the late summer sky. Gabe closed his eyes and listened. The lagoon was quiet, sleeping. There was nothing but the low buzz of cicadas and the occasional croak of a snoring frog.

The two kayakers paddled in silence, respecting the peace of the lagoon. After a crossing through another thin passageway, the lake opened up again, and Gabe spotted a small, round mound in the distance. "There it is," he said. "Dead Man's Island."

After the cozy tranquility of Lily Pad Lagoon, the vast open water felt cold and unstable. Haunted, even. They paddled quickly and kept their conversation going.

"My stepbrother is going to think this is the coolest adventure. As long as nothing nerdy happens to cancel it out."

"What do you mean?"

"I've got a logic proof," Gabe said. "I am trying to prove that I am not just a nerd who does only nerdy things. But so far I don't know if I can prove it. I've got a chart, and for every good adventure there is a geeky part."

"Like what?"

"Okay. Like our karaoke thing. That was pretty awesome, right? But we were singing all the countries of the world. That's nerdy, so it negates my hypothesis."

The bow of Gabe's kayak slid stiffly onto the sand of Dead Man's Island. Amanda's came ashore right next to his.

"You always look at things backward," she said.

Here we go again, Gabe thought. *Just like she always says it's me who's stalking her when it's really her stalking me. How is she going to turn this around?*

"We sang the countries of the world," Amanda said, "but we had a really crazy sing-off. So for every geeky thing, there's a really cool adventure."

Gabe turned to face her. He thought about the time his math team friends slept over his house and how they all looked a little different in the morning. Not just because they were wearing pajamas and orthodontic headgear, but because he had spent a whole night with them and felt like he knew them better than he did before. As the light from Gabe's hat shined into Amanda's face, he had the same thought about her. She was wearing a sweatshirt like any other and her hair was still long and thick and kind of wild in the light, but somehow she looked just a little bit different.

Amanda covered her face with her hands. "Are you trying to blind me?" she said.

Gabe moved his head back to face the island. "Do you really think someone died here?"

"I don't know."

Gabe unhooked his peanut butter jar from the bungee cords at the front of his boat and unscrewed the lid. It would have been easy to jump onto the island to scoop up the sand, but, thinking like Nikhil, he decided to scoop from within his kayak. Just to be safe. He turned the boat sideways, reached over the side, and scooped a big jarful of red sand.

"Oh, no!" Amanda cried.

"What?" Gabe pictured ghosts and dead bodies and long trails of blood.

"My cup is missing. I must have lost it when I lost my flashlight."

"Oh, come on," Gabe said.

"I'm serious. Good thing you brought a jar big enough for both of us."

Typical, Gabe thought as he screwed the cap on the heavy jar of red sand—*his* red sand that *he* had gotten by sneaking out and *not* getting caught in branches and *not* dropping his flashlight and jar into the water. Amanda was on the Blue team, and this was Color *War*, not Color Sharing. He'd already helped her enough that night. She'd still be stuck in the thicket and the dark if it weren't for him. Now she expected him to share his sand, too?

But there was something about the darkness and the hour and the talk they'd just had and the journey they'd just gone on—there was something that told him they were in this together.

"Yeah," Gabe said. "Good thing."

After paddling back and pulling the kayaks onto shore and sprinting across the field, and nudging Nikhil to tell him he was back, Gabe lay in his bed with his eyes closed and the sounds of camp wrapped around him. He'd made it.

Maybe Dead Man's Island *was* haunted. It had to be an otherworldly spirit that made him think Amanda looked different in that light and made him promise to share half his sand with her. She was on the Blue team, and she was annoying and crazy and always looking at things backward.

But maybe she was right about one thing. Even if he was a nerd, he had just had one awesome adventure.

Problem: Am I a nerd who only has nerdy adventures?

Hypothesis: No.

Proof:

THINGS I CAN TELL ZACK (I am not a nerd.)	THINGS I CAN'T TELL ZACK (I am a nerd.)
1. I'm going to sleepaway camp for six weeks!	1. It is the Summer Center for Gifted Enrichment.
2. My bunkmates are really cool, and we became friends right away!	2. They like learning digits of π.
3. The food is bad, just like at camps in ~~books and~~ movies!	3. We fixed it with lemon juice to kill the bacteria.
4. I'm being stalked by an annoying girl!	4. She is in my Logical Reasoning and Poetry Writing classes.
5. I creamed Amanda in a sing-off!	5. We sang all the countries of the world.
6. We put music and sports pictures on our walls.	6. They are of Beethoven and the rules of badminton.
7. Wesley says amazing things in his sleep!	7. He solves math problems. 7a. and brainteasers.
8. I tried some cool hairstyles that lots of girls said looked cute.	8. One is named for Julius Caesar.
9. Vampire lice are sucking the blood out of people's heads!	9. We learned all about the *Pediculus humanus capitis* and their life cycle.

225

THINGS I CAN TELL ZACK (I am not a nerd.)	THINGS I CAN'T TELL ZACK (I am a nerd.)
10. I discovered a top secret operation!	10. It was an operation to study the science of lice.
11. I hung out with the coolest guy at camp!	11. His nickname is C^2, and he is so smart, he skipped two grades.
12. Color War broke with aliens landing in the middle of the night!	12. Our algorithm was off by a few days.
13. Green won 90 points in field day!	13. A rocket crashed into the water-balloon toss because the teacher added too much calcium carbide.
14. We got ~~three five six~~ all of our scavenger hunt items.	14. They ~~are~~ include a simile, a metaphor, and a word from the dictionary.
15. A celebrity came to camp, and I got a picture with him!	15. He's the host of a game show for smart people.
16. ~~I'm going to kayak~~ I kayaked to Dead Man's Island in the middle of the night.	16. I read books about islands, I had a flashlight on my hat. . . . But does it matter?

Chapter 27

BACKWARD LOGIC

The next morning's breakfast was the last color-coded meal, and it sparked a realization of all the last things coming up. This was the last morning of Color War. After that would be the last few days of classes. Tonight, he and his bunkmates would learn their last digit of Pi. And Saturday was the last day of Summer Center. Six weeks of camp, over in a blink.

Gabe got a round of applause when he presented the red sand to C^2 during the designated scavenger hunt time. Maybe it was because he didn't want his teammates to know that he'd helped a Blue team member, or maybe it was because he was taking a cue from C^2, who accepted the cup of sand without asking any questions, but Gabe decided to keep most of the details about his journey private. Nikhil thought it safer if he didn't know the specifics of how his bunkmate broke the rules, and Wesley was impressed just knowing that it happened at all, so it wasn't too hard. Gabe had a flash of nervousness when he passed Amanda on the field, but all she did was shout, "Blue is the best!" When Jenny stuck her tongue out at him, he knew that Amanda hadn't told anyone about last night either.

The Color War battles ended with the scavenger hunt in the morning, but the official closing ceremony wasn't until after dinner. The administration spent the day tallying the scavenger hunt scores and divvying up points for sportsmanship and team spirit, and the campers had shortened sessions of each of their classes. They were only going to have two more days of school after this, and both Miss Carey and Mr. Justice said that those two days would be spent working on a final project to present to their families when they came to pick them up.

The return to school was like the landing of another UFO: the focus and atmosphere of the whole camp shifted instantly. Instead of scoreboards and giant maps and mud pits, the camp became filled with rocket launchpads and soil samples and even the beginnings of a replica of a medieval village. The excitement and competitive spirit was still there; it was just redirected.

Gabe sat on a tree stump, his hair brushed forward and flipped up in the front, thinking about his final poem. Mr. Justice had taken the class out to the woods for inspiration, but Gabe's wasn't coming. He knew he wanted to write about camp, but that could mean anything that happened in the last six weeks. It was so big that he didn't know how to start, and he had no idea which of all his memories were even worth writing about.

He'd had the same mental blank when thinking about his final logic proof. All he could think about was the personal logic proof he'd been working on all summer. He'd thought that all his adventures would prove that he wasn't a nerd, but they presented a stronger case for the opposite. Summer Center was one big adventure in geekdom. But was there any truth in what Amanda said? Did the geekdom part not necessarily cancel out the adventure?

Mr. Justice knelt down beside Gabe's stump. "How's it coming, Gabe?"

Gabe sighed. "I don't know what to write."

"Do you know which form you'd like to write in?" Mr. Justice asked. The final poem could be any type of poem they'd studied, and they'd studied lots.

"No," Gabe said. "Maybe a haiku or a sonnet."

Mr. Justice smiled. "You like meter."

Gabe nodded. He did like poems that had set rules about how many lines or words or syllables you could use. "You have to make it fit," he said. "Like the old wooden puzzles I had when I was little. There was this board with the outline, and you had to figure out which pieces went where to make it come together. Writing those poems is kind of like that."

Mr. Justice nodded. "Kind of like a logic problem."

"Yeah," Gabe said slowly. "It *is* kind of like a logic problem. . . ." Mr. Justice stood up and went to check in with someone else, leaving Gabe with all the neurons in his brain beginning to fire.

He had a flashback of Amanda last night, sitting opposite him in her kayak and saying, *You always look at things backward.* He could think of his poem like a logic problem . . . and his logic proof like a poem. Solving a logic problem meant taking a whole bunch of facts—givens—and combining them to come to one solution. But writing a poem was the opposite: You took a big thing—the woods, say—and broke it down into small things—the smell of the leaves, the sound of the wind.

Instead of looking at his nerd chart as a set of facts that needed to prove one thing or another, he began to look at it as a collection of memories and moments. When camp was over, he wouldn't have just one conclusion, he'd have all these fun and funny and crazy experiences. He could combine them to prove all sorts of different things or make any type of poem. And he'd remember every one of them—they were all *him*, more than any hairstyle was. He had a feeling he wouldn't be looking back at his logic proof anymore.

Amanda walked behind Gabe's stump and looked over his shoulder at his blank piece of paper. "I'm almost done already," she bragged.

Gabe looked up. "I'm just starting to get it."

Chapter 28

THE RESULTS

"I think we won," said Wesley.

"We should assume that we came in last place," said Nikhil. "That way, we'll be sure to be happy with whatever place we came in."

"We should *hope* we got first, though," said Gabe. His hair was not gelled at all, just plain and in need of a haircut.

"Hope it, okay," said Nikhil, "but be ready for any result, just in case."

"I'm ready to win," said Wesley.

The loudspeakers crackled and then began broadcasting the music of a violin quartet. It was a complicated, lively tune, and though some kids looked confused and one stood up and began to wave his arms as though he were conducting, everyone stopped talking to listen. A procession started onto the stage: first the teachers, then the nurse and librarian, then the administrators, and finally the director of the camp. The staff formed a line at the top of the stage, and the director stood in the center wearing a red hat, a green shirt, blue shorts, and knee-high yellow socks. The music stopped, and all the campers applauded. Then the staff on stage began applauding too, but pointing their hands at the campers.

"Welcome to the Color War closing ceremonies," the director said. "That wonderful music you just heard was *Color War Opus in E-flat*, composed and performed by Summer Center campers from four summers ago."

Everyone clapped again.

"Before I read the final scores and announce the winner," the director continued, "I'd like you all to give yourselves a HUGE round of applause. You all did an excellent job. What a stimulating, enriching, fun few days we've had!"

A couple of days ago, they all would have jumped to their feet and begun chanting cheers about their teams. But the scores were already tallied, and classes were already back in session. All anyone cared about now was the results.

"Without further ado," the director said, "I have the Color War results." She pulled out a multicolored envelope, and a whole roomful of bodies shifted closer to the edge of their seats. "The award for best sportsmanship goes to . . . the RED TEAM!"

The Red team cheered, but the other three teams cheered louder. Everyone knew the sportsmanship award never went to the team that had won.

"The award for best team spirit goes to . . . the YELLOW team!" In honor of the yellow team's sing-off performance, she added in a robotic voice, "Or should I say the 10010 team."

"We had to win it," Wesley said excitedly. "That leaves just us and Blue, and only *we* had red sand!"

Gabe swallowed but kept quiet. What were the odds that the red sand would make the difference between winning and losing, that his sharing with Amanda would push her team over the edge and leave Green in second place?

"And now for the final scores. In fourth place, with 470 points . . . is the RED team!"

The Red team was clearly bummed, and they stayed that way despite their counselors' pretending fourth was the best place to be.

"I'm going to have to announce the rest in a somewhat different way," the director said, "because we had something incredibly rare happen. We have two teams *tied* for second place, with 525 points each."

A symphony of murmers and whispers went through the crowd.

"But the winning team . . ."—the director paused and let the suspense hang there—"won us over with their team spirit and sportsmanship and fantastic sing-off performance. With 655 points, it's the YELLOW team!"

The yellow team sprang to their feet and began screaming and jumping on top of one another.

"Tied for second," Nikhil said proudly. "I was expecting fourth."

Wesley kicked the seat in front of him. "I can't believe we came in second. And that we tied with Blue."

"At least we beat Red," Gabe said, resigned. "And they knew about the milk snake."

Wesley covered his eyes. "Watch out, Gabe. Here comes Amanda Wisznewski, and she's probably going to say we copied her by coming in second."

Gabe couldn't help but laugh, even as he shook his head.

What she should do was thank him; if he hadn't shared his sand, Blue would be third to Green's second. But she probably would say exactly what Wesley predicted.

She tapped him on the shoulder. "We tied. You know what that means," she said.

Gabe and Wesley and Nikhil waited.

Amanda smiled. "We're meant to be."

Chapter 29

THE SURPRISE

With the row of packed bags along the wall—Gabe's suitcase between Wesley's duffel and Nikhil's trunk—Gabe felt like he'd stepped out of a time machine into the first day of camp. How strange to think that only six weeks ago, he had just arrived at Summer Center and didn't know Wesley or Nikhil or Amanda or the postulates of logical reasoning or the difference between a couplet and a triolet.

The three of them were mostly done packing, but they'd decided to leave all their pictures and lists and graphs on the walls until after their parents came. Even Nikhil agreed that being able to hold on to the feeling that the bunk was still theirs outweighed the risk of not being 100 percent packed by the time the parents arrived. Stark white walls would have been too sad. And besides, they wanted to show off their Pi digits and Wesley's sleeping-bag times and their celebrity photos and the funny things they all said. They'd spent the first hour of the allotted packing time reading their walls and reliving the memories. It was only when David knocked on their wall and said that families would begin arriving in an hour—and then they'd need to go get lunch before their class presentations at one o'clock—that they got to work.

Wesley found a lump of clothes wedged between his bed frame and the wall. "I didn't realize I brought this shirt," he said. He shrugged, blew a ball of dust off it, and stuffed it into his duffel bag.

"That bag is so big," said Gabe, "you could put a body in there."

"I do have a body in it," said Wesley seriously. "A *body of knowledge* about geometry and Shakespeare!"

All three of them cracked up.

Nikhil sighed and sat down on his bare mattress. "I wish school was going to be like Summer Center."

"I know!" said Gabe. "This is like school, but even more fun."

"And the other kids don't make fun of you," said Wesley.

"And they don't call you a nerd and teacher's pet," said Nikhil.

"Or say SCGE stands for Smart Camp for Geeks and Eggheads."

"That's what they called it at my school too!" said Nikhil.

"Who called it that?" Gabe asked.

"Everyone," said Wesley. "My mom came into school and told my teacher that I was going here, and then my teacher announced it to the class."

"My mom told Julia Renderson's mom," Nikhil said through gritted teeth, "and then Julia told *everyone*, and they started calling it that."

"Smart Camp for Geeks and Eggheads . . . That's pretty good for people who aren't smart enough to come here," Gabe said. "I bet my stepbrother would call it that too. But you know what? Even if we are nerds, we did a lot of really cool stuff."

"Well, *duh*," said Wesley. "That's because this camp is awesome."

"Yeah!" said Nikhil. "Even if it is Smart Camp for Geeks and Eggheads."

"I get to be Geek!" called Wesley.

"No," said Nikhil. "Gabe should be Geek because his name starts with *G*."

"I'm Geek," said Gabe proudly.

"Okay," said Wesley. "Then I'm Smarty, and Nikhil's Egghead."

"I don't want to be Egghead," said Nikhil. "Besides, your head is kind of shaped like an egg. Gabe, don't you think Wesley's head is shaped like an egg?"

"Is it?" asked Wesley seriously.

Gabe cocked his head. "Kind of. If eggs had hair and wore glasses."

"I can see eggs wearing glasses," said Wesley, "but imagine if they had hair. Nasty."

They all laughed. "That goes on the quote wall," said Nikhil. He got up, took a pencil out of his pocket, and added it to the long list of funny things they'd said or heard during the past six weeks.

"Hey, can I use your pencil?" said Gabe. A proud Geek, he walked to the drawing of the three of them that they'd had made during the caricatures activity. He used the pencil to write in their names below their faces: SMARTY, GEEK, AND EGG-HEAD. Then he added, THE WORLD'S COOLEST NERDS.

From the front of the cabin, David shouted, "It's noon, guys! Families will begin arriving any minute now. Make sure you're all packed!"

As sad as he was to leave Summer Center, the sound of the word "family" made Gabe think about how long it had been since he'd seen his mom. He hoped she'd be the first to arrive.

"I can't wait to see my family," said Nikhil. "Even my sister."

"My stepbrother told me my mom is bringing me a surprise," said Gabe. "But I have no idea what it is."

"My grandparents are coming," said Wesley. "And my mom and dad and brother and sister. And my aunt and uncle who are visiting from China." He scratched his egg-shaped head. "I hope there's room for me in the car."

"And for your body of knowledge," said Nikhil.

"Why are so many people coming to pick you up?" Gabe asked.

Wesley grinned. "They're my Fans. Get it? Because my last name is Fan."

As if on cue, the first family through the cabin door was

the Fans, and there were a lot of them. "Dad!" shouted Wesley. He flew off his top bunk into the arms of a man who looked just like he did, only taller and with graying hair. Then Wesley was swallowed up by hugs and kisses and a flurry of conversation in Chinese. Wesley's brother and sister began squeezing between and climbing over their relatives to walk around and look at the walls. There was hardly any room to fit them all, and Gabe could see that Nikhil was probably thinking about fire hazards, so he suggested he and Nikhil go wait for their families outside.

The campground was swarming with people, and more and more were parading over the hill to the bunk area in large clumps led by counselors and staff.

"There's my mom!" shouted Nikhil. He sprinted toward an oncoming group of families and was greeted by a tall, thin Indian couple. Gabe watched as a small girl with long pigtails jumped out from between Nikhil's parents and tackled Nikhil to the ground. They rolled down the hill in a tangle of arms and legs. Nikhil jumped to his feet and brushed himself off, but the girl kept rolling—making other families jump over her or step out of her way—until she landed close to Gabe. She stood up and showed off a smile that was missing so many teeth, it looked like a chess-board. Gabe wondered how many she'd lost naturally and how many she'd lost doing things like tackling Nikhil and rolling down hills.

When Nikhil and his parents reached the cabin, Nikhil said, "This is one of my bunkmates, Gabe. And this is my mom and my dad and my sister, Mo. She's the crazy person who could have gotten hurt rolling down the hill."

"I love danger," said Mo, smiling devilishly.

Gabe laughed. He couldn't imagine how one family could have two children who were such opposites.

Nikhil's family went into the cabin, and Wesley's came out shortly after. Gabe tried to be patient, but he was disappointed every time someone rounded the hill who wasn't his mom. Wesley's family came back out of the cabin and began talking to him. Talking to them all made Gabe wish he had more people coming to get him. Maybe not as many as Wesley had, but just a little more than his mom. He felt a familiar pang of yearning for a sibling. *I will have a sibling in a few weeks*, he reminded himself. *Once I go back home.*

Someone tapped Gabe on the shoulder. He whirled around. "Mom!"

"Gabe, honey!" She wrapped him in her arms. "I missed you!" she said, squeezing a bit tighter on the word *missed*.

"Me too. But I have so much to show you and—" Gabe broke away from his mother's hug and saw his surprise.

"Hey, man!" said Zack.

Gabe blinked a few times behind his glasses. "Whoa," he said.

"Are you surprised?" his mom asked.

"Yeah," Gabe said honestly. He was also nervous and confused and angry. He was going to stop pretending around Zack from now on—he was sure about that—but he wasn't sure he was ready for Zack to see his camp for what it really was. He worked hard all summer to keep Zack from finding out the truth about Summer Center. Now that Zack was here—*here at camp*—he didn't know what would happen.

"It seems like you had the most awesome summer ever," Zack said. "Now that I live in New York, I had to come see where it all went down."

Maybe he won't figure it out, Gabe thought desperately. "Yeah, cool. Hey, Zack!"

"Is this your bunk, honey?" asked Gabe's mom. "Can we go inside and see?"

"Um, sure." Gabe led them into the cabin and down the length of it. They squeezed past other kids and their parents, including Nikhil's family. Gabe would have introduced them, but Nikhil's sister was leaping from one top bunk to another, and Nikhil was focused on telling her to come down, so Gabe decided to do it later. "This is my section," he said when they reached it. "I shared it with Wesley and Nikhil."

"Is this them?" Zack asked. He walked right up to the caricature that now said, in Gabe's handwriting, SMARTY, GEEK, AND EGGHEAD: THE WORLD'S COOLEST NERDS.

Gabe had to remind himself to breathe. "Yeah, that's the three of us," he said as nonchalantly as possible. He took off his glasses and began rubbing out an imaginary smudge with his shirt. He had to prepare himself to see Zack's reaction as he took in the rest of the room. He put his glasses back on as his mom was commenting on the READING ROCKS poster and Zack was examining the funny quote board, which also contained flashes of genius they didn't want to forget, like "Good idea for a comic book about two gangs: Similes vs. Metaphors" and "Good invention: Windshield wipers for glasses."

"What's a sim-mile?" asked Zack.

Gabe looked where he was pointing. "Oh, a simile?" he said. "That's a comparison that uses the word 'like' or 'as.' I learned about them in my Poetry Writing class."

Wesley ran back into the room to grab a hat. "And in Color War," he said. "We needed a simile for the scavenger hunt, and we used 'The lake was as cold as an ice age.'"

"Oh," said Zack, his forehead wrinkled beneath his spiky black hair. "And who's that?" He pointed to a printout on the wall near the ceiling.

Wesley stopped, his mouth in a circle. "That's Beethoven! You don't know Beethoven?"

"Oh," said Zack. "He was a president, right?"

Wesley's jaw dropped even lower.

"Of course he knows Beethoven," said Gabe quickly. "The composer. He's just kidding around."

"Yeah," said Zack, looking at Gabe with a combination of gratitude and befuddlement.

Gabe's mom smiled and pulled Gabe toward her to kiss the top of his head.

Wesley started laughing. "You really had me!" he said to Zack. "Beethoven a president! He wasn't even American! But he does kind of look like Andrew Jackson. I always thought that."

Gabe tapped his nose. "Just the hair," he said.

"Oh, yeah," said Zack sarcastically. "They could be hair twins."

Wesley cracked up. "You're funny," he said, "like Gabe! And your hair is kind of like the kind of hair he had for a while."

Gabe's mom looked at Gabe with her eyebrows raised, but her eyes were smiling.

"Let's go to lunch," Wesley said, leading the way out of the bunk. "I hope it's not lemon-plasma oatmeal again! Remember that?"

Gabe laughed. They had first had lemon-plasma oatmeal on the very first morning of camp. That felt like ages ago. His mom walked ahead, listening to Wesley tell her about how Nikhil taught them to put lemon juice on their food to kill bacteria.

"Lemon-plasma oatmeal?" said Zack, staying back. He looked up at the banner with Pi to the twentieth digit. "What kind of camp is this?" he asked.

Gabe looked at himself and Zack, nerd and non. He'd known this moment was bound to happen, only he'd imagined it happening when he was back home and had had more

247

time to prepare. But in a way, hadn't he had this whole summer to prepare?

He thought about Amanda, who he even sort of liked, despite her being so annoying and getting everything backward. And he thought about Nikhil and his sister, who were complete opposites but clearly loved each other anyway.

He took a deep breath. "SCGE stands for Summer Center for Gifted Enrichment," he said. "It's a camp for nerds."

Zack's shoulders drew up, and he cocked his head, taking this in. "But all the stuff you wrote about. Like kayaking to Dead Man's Island—"

"I kind of can't believe I did that," said Gabe.

"And the lice—"

Gabe shuddered, remembering.

"And Color War. All that happened *here*, at"—he looked at the drawing of SMARTY, GEEK, AND EGGHEAD—"at this camp?"

Gabe nodded proudly. "And I didn't even write to you about some of the best parts. Come on, I'll tell you at lunch."

Chapter 30

THE SHORTCUT

The bunkmates and their families sat together in the cafeteria. The boys recounted their favorite camp moments, telling their families all about Alex Trebek and the lice lab and Gabe's karaoke stardom.

Gabe and his mom chatted happily, Wesley's siblings asked endless questions about his summer, and Nikhil's sister tried walking back from the buffet with her tray balanced on her head, which had Nikhil panicking. But Zack didn't talk to anyone. Gabe could see him taking it all in, occasionally rolling his eyes, and stabbing at his food almost angrily. The only thing holding him back from making fun of the nerdiness of it all was probably that the parents were there.

Who cares what Zack thinks? Gabe told himself. But he still barely ate, even though his tray was filled with delicious impress-the-parents food. As much as his brain insisted it didn't matter, his heart knew that it did.

After lunch, all the families paraded out of the cafeteria and toward classrooms for the presentations.

"Where's the lake?" Zack asked. "And the kayaks?"

"I can show you," Gabe said, happy to hear Zack talk and anxious to show him something Gabe knew he'd find cool. "Mom," he said. He had to say it a few times to get her attention; she was absorbed in conversation with Nikhil's parents. "Zack and I are going to go this way so I can show him the lake."

"You two go ahead, honey," she said. "I'll meet you at the math building."

"Come on," said Gabe. He cut away from the mass of people and scooted to the right, toward the woods. "You can actually get to the lake from the field, but this is a good shortcut."

As he led the way through the woods, Gabe kept talking, rambling on about how great kayaking was, to avoid Zack's silent, piercing judgment. Running ahead meant he didn't have to see Zack's expression, but he could hear Zack behind him, dodging trees, crumpling dead leaves, and jumping over roots.

"I can't believe the summer is almost over," Gabe said, "and the wedding is really soon and you already moved to New York. The lake is just up here." Gabe slowed down, but he didn't hear Zack. He glanced over his shoulder. "Zack?"

Zack was about twenty feet away. His body was as stiff as a sheet of ice, and his face was just as drained of color. His arms were up near his chest, and his fingers were spread wide.

"What is it?" Gabe asked.

Zack's lower lip began to tremble. "Snake," he said quietly, his voice rattling. "Snake. Snake. Snake." With each "snake," his breathing became heavier and his body began shaking more, until he was trembling all over and almost hysterical.

"Snake?" Gabe inhaled sharply and his body tensed up. "Where?"

Zack motioned with his chin. "R-right there. By this log."

Gabe took a cautious step forward. The snake moved. Zack screamed.

The snake curled itself over the log, and Gabe gasped

again. It was a snake all right, long as a yardstick but very slender. Its body was beige, like the log, but covered with thick, bloodred bands. Gabe's eyes began to widen. He dared to lean ever-so-slightly closer to get a better look. Just as he'd hoped, the red marks weren't stripes; they were blotches, and they were outlined in black. He'd recognize that snake anywhere.

"It's an eastern milk snake!" he said.

Zack moved his eyes from the snake for the first time, to look at Gabe like he'd just suggested they invite the snake to dinner. "Who cares, you nerd!" he yelled. "It's going to kill us!"

"No! Eastern milk snakes are harmless," Gabe explained. "I know it for a fact. And that's an eastern milk snake. I'm positive."

The eastern milk snake moved its tail end rapidly, making the leaves swish, and both boys jumped back. Then it stuck its head in the air and slithered along the log.

"It's okay. It's harmless," Gabe repeated coolly, both for Zack's benefit and his own. "One hundred percent harmless."

"How do you know?" Zack asked. His body was starting to thaw, but his eyes were still trained on the snake, which was now stretched out along the top of the log. It looked like it could slither into the woods, away from camp, if only some-one gave it a nudge.

"It was the Final *Jeopardy!* question in our Color War *Jeopardy!*" Gabe slowly, deliberately bent down. He picked up a long stick. "It's a harmless snake, native to this region but rarely seen at camp." He took small, light steps toward the log. The snake didn't move. "And it sounds like it goes with your breakfast cereal."

"Breakfast cereal?" said Zack. He stared, with awe and fear, as Gabe reached the stick out toward the snake.

"Milk snake. Cereal and milk."

Harmless, Gabe reminded himself one last time. He poked the snake with the stick. Both boys held their breath.

The milk snake adjusted itself as though it was tired but knew it had to wake up. Gabe poked it again. This time, it slithered slowly down, off the log and into the woods. When the very tip of its tail was out of sight, Gabe closed his eyes and let out a deep sigh.

Zack laughed nervously. "Cereal and milk," he said.

Gabe snickered.

The two boys stood there, staring at each other from opposite sides of the log, laughing out of relief.

"I'm so glad you knew that was harmless," said Zack, "or else I would've totally freaked out."

Gabe raised his eyebrows. "*Would* have?" he said.

Zack rolled his eyes and shrugged one shoulder. "Okay, I guess I did freak out a little."

"A little?" Gabe said.

After glancing into the woods to make sure the snake was gone, Zack hopped the log and gave Gabe a light punch in the shoulder. His arm was still shaking. "Okay, I was really scared. But you weren't! You went up and poked it with that stick!"

Gabe shrugged and felt himself blush. "I knew it was harmless from camp *Jeopardy!*"

"Man," Zack said, shaking his head and smiling. "I don't know what would've happened if you weren't such a nerd."

Gabe tried to think of something Zack might say. "No biggie. It's cool." And it was.

Chapter 31

FAMILY

"And then," said Zack as Carla buttoned his tuxedo jacket, "the snake kind of hissed at Gabe, but he didn't even flinch!"

"It didn't really hiss," said Gabe. He stepped up next to his dad, who was tying his bow tie in front of the long dressing-room mirror. "But he did move his tail around in the leaves, and it sort of sounded like a rattlesnake, which was scary."

"But Gabe wasn't even scared! He just said, 'Dude, this is a milk snake'—"

"Eastern milk snake."

"'This is an eastern milk snake, and it's harmless!' And

then he got a stick and poked it. And the snake looked like it wanted to attack—"

"Well, it really just looked like it was yawning."

"And Gabe poked it again! And then it slithered away. And then we went to Gabe's logic class, and he told his teacher that we saw a milk snake, and the teacher used a walkie-talkie to tell the camp director, and then everyone was talking about it."

"It was the first time someone's seen a milk snake on the campgrounds in over twenty years. The Animal Science teacher was really jealous and wanted me to show her exactly where we saw it, so she could go looking for it."

Zack joined Gabe and his dad in front of the mirror. "And when we walked to his other class, all these girls were saying hi to Gabe like he was a celebrity."

Gabe blushed. "They just knew me from karaoke and the hairstyles activity."

"And this girl Amanda kept telling everyone that she was the snake killer's best friend."

Gabe shook his head. "Amanda Wisznewski."

Zack went to stand behind his mom, who was putting on her lipstick. "And then, in his poetry class," Zack said, "everyone read poems that they wrote, and Gabe's was the best one! The rhymes were all really good, and it was all about camp, but he didn't have anything about the snake in it because he wrote it before we saw the snake."

Carla smiled at the two boys with her newly red lips. "I'm so proud of you, Gabe," she said. "Both of you, for being so brave."

Gabe's dad bent down and touched Gabe's hair, which was gelled just like Zack's. "And I'm just as proud of you both as I was the first time I heard the story," he said, giving Gabe a kiss on the forehead. "And the second. And the third."

Carla laughed and took off the apron she was wearing over her wedding dress. Her sister, Zack's aunt, helped pin a short, white veil into her hair. "It is a great story," said Carla. "I'm not tired of it yet."

"You had to see this snake, Mom," said Zack. "It had these red spots all over it."

"Outlined in black," said Gabe. "That's what made me sure it was an eastern milk snake."

"He knew it from camp *Jeopardy!*" said Zack.

"I invited the snake to the wedding," Gabe's dad said. "But he had a prior engagement."

Gabe and Zack cracked up.

"But are my two best men ready?" Gabe's dad asked. "Some people are waiting for us to get married."

"Okay," said Zack. "We'll tell you the rest later."

The four of them held hands as they walked to line up for the wedding ceremony. Gabe knew that this was just the beginning.

Chapter 32

BACK HOME

Awake, with his eyes closed and the lights out, Gabe absorbed the night back in his own bed. School started in the morning, which meant the summer was officially coming to a close. What a summer it had been.

The sound of crickets coming through the open window was quieter than it was at camp, and despite the breeze the air was stickier. He smelled coffee rather than grease, and since his mom had already shut off the TV and gone up to her room, there were no distant voices like the counselors in the clearing.

Gabe put on his glasses to look at the time. 12:02 a.m. It

was later than when he'd snuck out of bed to kayak to Dead Man's Island, but not as late as when the UFO landed and broke Color War, or as late as he and Zack had stayed up the night of the wedding. He wondered if Wesley was talking in his sleep right then and if Nikhil was starting a new book at the end to make sure it worked out okay.

He took off his glasses and tried once again to fall asleep. But after a few minutes, he put them on again and got out of bed. He tiptoed downstairs and jiggled the mouse to wake up the computer. Pressing lightly on the keys so as not to make any noise, he started to type a letter that he'd print out and send to four people: Nikhil, Wesley, Amanda, and Zack.

I don't really have anything to write about yet because school only starts tomorrow. But I'll keep writing and telling you everything, especially the nerdy stuff! You have to write back!!

I was so busy with the wedding that I didn't get to send you a copy of my final poem like I promised. Here it is.

A Camp Sonnet

I know some people wouldn't think it's cool
To go to camp at the SCGE,
Because you're spending summertime in school
And learning logic proofs and poetry.

It's true that here we exercise our minds
And sing about the countries of the Earth
And learn past the 19th digit of Pi
And build a lab to study lice's birth.

A rocket crashed our field day like a bird,
And Wesley did his math asleep at night.
Some people think these givens make us nerds.
At first I worried logic proved them right.

BUT

If NERD CAMP's what you call 6 weeks of fun,
That only proves that nerds are number one!

Get ready to geek out ... s'more!

Turn the page for a sneak peek at
what next summer holds for Gabe and Zack
in NERD CAMP 2.0.

The main difference between Zack and his stepbrother, Gabe, could be summed up by baseball cards: Zack collected baseball cards to trade with his friends, while Gabe slid baseball cards under the strap of his night brace to prevent the headgear from itching his skull.

When Zack first saw that Gabe had brought baseball cards with him for his weekend in New York City, he was surprised and impressed. The stepbrothers finally had something in common. "You collect?" Zack asked. "Want to trade?"

"That'd be good," said Gabe. "Mine are starting to get permanent indents, and that defeats the purpose."

"What do you mean?" Zack asked.

Gabe took his night brace out of his duffel bag and wrapped it around his head, hooking it to pieces of metal on either side of his teeth. He then slid five baseball cards underneath the strap, from one ear to the other. "See?" he said. "I need to wear this whenever I'm at home, and all night. The fabric itches, though, so I put the cards underneath. An added bonus is that the cards keep my hair from getting too creased."

"Dude," said Zack. "With that thing on, I don't think anybody's looking at your hair."

"Ha-ha," said Gabe, removing the cards but not the headgear. "What do you do with your baseball cards, then?"

"I collect them," Zack said. "See?" He took out a small binder that was filled with pages of plastic sleeves. In each sleeve was a baseball card, and not one was creased or dented in any way. "My best ones are up front here, and they get worse as you go back. But sometimes I mix it up. I put some good ones toward the back so people won't know if I'm trying to give them my worst cards."

"What makes a card good or bad?" Gabe asked.

"Lots of things, like how good the player is, or if the card is rare. Some rare ones can be worth a ton of money, especially if they're old."

Gabe squinted through his bifocals and turned a couple of pages of the binder. "These look pretty new."

"Yeah, nobody can really afford old ones, since they're so expensive. Except for Leighton Ayres, who won't even trade with anyone because none of our cards are good enough for him." Zack rolled his eyes. "But my friend Nick found all these boxes of old cards in his basement, and his dad sold them for hundreds of bucks. That's what got everyone at school into collecting. And all those old cards were once new."

"Everything old was once new," Gabe said with wonder. "I'm taking a research methods class at camp this summer, and the first step of the scientific method is to make observations. That's a really good observation. Think about it. Really old books were once new books in stores. My mom's old camera that takes pictures on actual film, that was new once, and people probably thought it was really cool and the best way to take pictures. And artifacts! Think about those old pots at the Museum of Natural History. They were once new pots that people used for cooking."

Zack didn't understand why Gabe always had to think

about things so deeply. All he meant was that if he collected baseball cards now, eventually his new cards would be old cards that were worth money. But Gabe had to go off and talk about nerdy things like books and film cameras and pots at the ancient history museum.

When his mom first married Gabe's dad, Zack found it weird when Gabe did stuff like that, which was most of the time. It was bad enough that Zack had to move all the way across the country, leaving his friends and his dad in California to live in New York City. Their apartment was even smaller than it had been in LA, it took an hour and two trains to get to the beach, and his new school had kids who'd been in class together since kindergarten. If he had to get a step-brother and make his family even more complicated, that stepbrother could at least be a built-in friend.

Looking back, it seemed stupid, but Zack had given a lot of thought to impressing his new stepbrother. He'd per-fected his skateboard moves, set new high scores on his video games, and combed through his iPod, imagining himself going through Gabe's and finding all the same songs. Then he met Gabe. Gabe, who couldn't balance on a skateboard, who preferred books to video games, and who hadn't heard of a single band Zack liked. Nothing would have made the move easy, but was it too much to ask that Gabe be *a little* like him?

Now that they'd been stepbrothers for almost a whole year, Zack still thought Gabe liked nerdy things, but he was more used to it. That was just Gabe. He was on a math team (which Zack still didn't get, since math wasn't a sport) and went to a special summer camp that was like school, only with even more learning. But he was also fun and funny, and his nerdiness could be useful, like if you needed help with your homework or if you ran into a snake in the woods and needed to know if it was poisonous or not, which had really happened last summer. People made fun of nerds at school, but Zack liked hanging out with Gabe despite the geeky things he said and did. There was even something admirable about the way Gabe didn't try to hide that he was a nerd—not that he could hide it if he tried. Here he was doing something normal like looking at baseball cards, yet he was wearing headgear and talking about artifacts.

"Dude," said Zack. "Take off that night brace."

"Oh! I didn't even realize I was still wearing it. Good observation!" said Gabe. The metal on his teeth reflected into Zack's eyes as he unhooked the headgear from his braces and placed it on Zack's TV, which served as Gabe's nightstand when he visited. "It's actually not that uncomfortable, apart from the itchy strap. Last week my mom let me ride my bike up to the Italian ices place at night to meet Eric and Ashley, and I did the same thing. I passed these kids from school on the way and they laughed at me, but I didn't realize why until I got there and Ashley told me I was wearing it. It was pretty embarrassing."

"Did you have the baseball cards around the back too?" Zack asked.

"Yeah," Gabe said. Then he brightened. "At least my hair wasn't creased!"

Zack shook his head in disbelief. If that had happened to him, he'd beg his mom to let him move back to California. He made a silent promise to himself that when he got braces—which his mom said was going to happen in the fall, despite all his protesting—he'd put up with the braces and that's it. If the orthodontist tried to make him wear headgear or put on rubber bands or crank his teeth with a metal key every day, he'd flat out refuse. If that didn't work, he'd keeping "losing" his orthodontic equipment until his mom and the doctor got the picture.

Gabe sat down on the edge of Zack's bed. "What's the status of Mission: Campossible?" he asked.

"It's good!" said Zack. He was so pleased with Gabe's help in trying to get him permission to go to sleepaway camp that summer, he didn't even mind that Gabe had given their plan such a cheesy name. Without Gabe's help, all Zack would have done was beg and tell his mom that everyone else was allowed to go to camp, and he didn't think that would have swayed her to let him go. No begging would have changed the fact that he was still only eleven, and for some reason his mom had it in her head that he couldn't go until he was twelve. Gabe, however, was full of ideas, and he knew how to do fancy research that impressed adults. "I think all the stuff we've been doing is working," Zack said.

"Tell me!" Gabe said.

"Well," Zack said, "she really liked that list you helped me make, about how camp makes you a maturer person."

"The Camp-Builds-Character Proof," Gabe said proudly.

"Right," said Zack. "And last night I told her about all the camps we found that are right near yours, and I said how that'd make it easy to drop us off and pick us up together."

"Did the map help?" Gabe asked. He'd plotted the

locations of five camps near his own on a map to show just how close they were.

"Yeah, the map totally helped," Zack said. "Thanks, man."

"No biggie," said Gabe. "I've been working on one more thing, and I think it'll be the clincher." He made a drumroll noise on his duffel bag, then removed and unfolded a poster-size chart filled with numbers.

"Whoa," said Zack. "What's that?"

"Remember I asked you about all the stuff you'd do this summer if you didn't go to camp? Well, I added up the esti-mated cost of all those things, and then I compared the total to the average cost of going to sleepaway camp. I think the numbers speak for themselves."

Zack sat on the bed next to Gabe. He never knew why people said numbers spoke for themselves; he usually needed a teacher to speak for them. And even then he had a hard time listening, since there was so much other, more interesting stuff he could be thinking about, like what time it was in California, or how to perfect his boardslide at the skate park, or what color the hardened gum on the bottom of his desk might be. So he couldn't completely understand how Gabe's chart worked, but he saw lists of things that, he had to admit, would make an awesome summer: extra guitar lessons, a new skateboard, going to the beach and renting a surfboard every weekend, buying new video games, flying to LA to visit his dad. "This shows how much all this stuff would cost?" he asked.

"Yep," said Gabe. "I didn't know you collected baseball cards. I should add that to the list. But even without it, all the stuff you'd do at home adds up to a lot more than six weeks at sleepaway camp. I think your mom and my dad will see that the cost-effective approach is to let you go to camp."

"You mean it's cheaper to send me to camp than make me stay home?"

Gabe nodded. "Good observation."

Zack pulled the chart closer to him and punched Gabe in the arm. "Dude!" he said. "My mom is going to flip. Here's an observation: You're the best!"

"Thank you." Gabe said, beaming. He rubbed his arm. "And ouch."

After his weekend with Zack, Gabe did the first thing he always did when he got back home: He gave his mom a big hug. He used to do it when he met his mom at Penn Station, but just as he was starting to feeling embarrassed about hugging his mom in the middle of New York City—where kids younger than him rode the subway without any parents—Gabe's mom decided that he was old enough to take the train from Penn Station back to Long Island by himself. He now first saw her in the car, and it was hard to hug someone who was sitting in the driver's seat, so he saved his big hug for right after they walked in the door of their house, but before he put down his duffel bag.

He was glad to be able to hug her in private, but he was also just glad to hug her. Even though it had only been one weekend, he always missed his mom while he was away. He loved spending time with his dad, and he liked his step-mom, Carla, just fine, but things were *different* there. The rules weren't as strict, for one thing. Gabe could drink as much soda as he wanted all day, not just one small glass when eating dinner at a restaurant. And he and Zack had a TV in their room, with cable and everything, which they could watch late at night or use to play video games. Gabe couldn't figure out why—and he'd spent a lot of time on the train trying—but for some reason it was easier to be at home, where he wasn't allowed to do as much.

"I missed you, Gabe," his mom said as they finished their hug. "What am I going to do when you're at Summer Center for six weeks?"

"I don't know," Gabe said. He dropped his duffel bag onto the floor and sat down on the couch. "But you have only fifty-eight days to figure it out."

"You leave for camp in fifty-eight days? I didn't know you were counting down."

"Fifty-eight days. Wesley's keeping track of hours and

Nikhil's counting minutes, so if you want to know more specifically, I can call them."

"That's okay," his mom said. "I don't think I could handle knowing how many hours. Though while you're gone, I may have to count the minutes until you get back." She gave him a kiss.

"Mom," Gabe said with a groan.

"You're right," she said. "Let's end this love fest so you can go unpack. Dirty clothes straight in the hamper, please."

Gabe e-mailed Wesley and Nikhil for the latest hour and minute update anyway. Thinking about camp made him wish he was there right now. His camp, the Summer Center for Gifted Enrichment, was like heaven. It was kind of like being at the gifted program at school, only without any non-GT kids walking by the door with their fingers in an L for "losers." And camp was every day and all day, from the morning wake-up siren until lights-out—or even overnight, since last summer his bunkmate Wesley solved math problems out loud in his sleep! This summer Gabe would be taking classes called "Research Methods" and "Heroes of Our World and Imaginations," which were sure to be stimulating. But the absolute best part—and there were lots and lots of next-best parts—was that everyone there was like Gabe. Last summer he'd spent a lot of time analyzing his camp adventures to determine whether or not Zack would find them nerdy. This summer he was determined to just relax and enjoy being surrounded by unashamedly geeky geeks.

Gabe thought more about Zack as he sorted his clothes into the white, light, and dark bins. He'd wanted a sibling forever, and having Zack didn't disappoint. Zack was super cool but also nice, and they always laughed a lot and did fun things together. Gabe wasn't as nervous about looking like a nerd now as he had been when he first met Zack; the first time they met he had to watch his every word, and all last summer he went to extremes to make sure Zack thought he was at a regular sleepaway camp, not what Zack would call "nerd camp."

Back then, Gabe thought as he dropped a pair of jeans in the pile of darks, it was like Zack was a white T-shirt and Gabe was a pair of dark jeans. Zack wouldn't dare mix with someone like Gabe. But now it was more like Zack was still the cool, crisp white shirt, but Gabe was the light blue shirt he was putting in the middle pile. He didn't have to hide the truth, but he was still constantly aware that he wasn't on Zack's level, so he tried not to act *too* nerdy during their weekends together. He'd brought his night brace and baseball cards, for instance, but he only put them on right before shutting off the light, instead of wearing them whenever he was home, like the orthodontist instructed. And when Zack talked about using his baseball cards for trading, Gabe didn't mention that a lot of his friends were into trading Element Cards; he knew Zack would find it geeky to try to collect cards to fill the entire periodic table. He noticed that Zack never invited other friends to hang out with them in Manhattan, but then again, the one time Zack came to visit Gabe on Long Island, Gabe didn't invite friends from school over either.

Summer Center, on the other hand, was like the whole pile of darks. There were kids who were as different as dark jeans and red shirts and striped pajamas, but they were all in a happy pile together. They all loved learning, and the coolest kids were the ones who loved learning the most. During class, they could speed through lessons because everyone caught on quickly, and the questions kids asked made the discussions deeper, not repetitive. During free time, campers memorized digits of pi and cracked jokes about history and turned a head lice epidemic into a science project. They'd probably all bring Element Cards this summer. Nobody worried about being a nerd, because Summer Center was nerd paradise.

According to the e-mails he'd gotten from Wesley and Nikhil, they'd all be there in fifty-eight days, twelve hours, and forty-two minutes. It couldn't come soon enough.

Something strange is happening at Mumpley Middle School. . . .

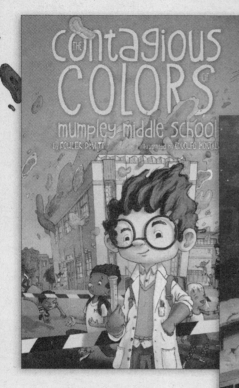

by FOWLER DeWITT

illustrated by RODOLFO MONTALVO